STAY ALIVE

F L O O D

STAY ALIVE

FLOOD

JOSEPH MONNINGER

SCHOLASTIC INC.

No part of this publication may be reproduced, stored in a retrieval system, or transmitted in any form or by any means, electronic, mechanical, photocopying, recording, or otherwise, without written permission of the publisher. For information regarding permission, write to Scholastic Inc., Attention: Permissions Department, 557 Broadway, New York, NY 10012.

ISBN 978-0-545-56359-8

All rights reserved. Published by Scholastic Inc., *Publishers since 1920.* SCHOLASTIC and associated logos are trademarks and/or registered trademarks of Scholastic Inc.

12 11 10 9 8 7 6 5 4 3 2 1   14 15 16 17 18 19/0

Printed in the U.S.A.   40
First printing, October 2014

FIRST AID

SURVIVAL TIP #1

Unfortunately, many modern homes fail to have on hand a useful first aid kit. The basic home first aid kit is the initial line of defense in any catastrophe. Although the practical benefits of a small medical supply kit (including a variety of bandages, tape, tweezers, scissors, hydrogen peroxide, and anything else one might find in a typical home medicine cabinet) are obvious to everyone, a well-stocked first aid kit should also contain several flashlights, a mirror, fire-making ingredients, water purification tablets, and a compass. These additional items take up little space, but they reward their inclusion by multiples of ten. Instead of thinking of a first aid kit as a "kit," think instead of a first aid, or disaster, backpack. Keep it fully stocked and hang it in a handy place. One grab should be all it takes for any member of the family to meet the basic demands of an emergency.

CHAPTER 1

Kuru Elcock, 13, stuck her head in the back room of the Lincoln Bakery on River Street in Marseilles, Illinois, and waited for her eyes to adjust. It took a moment to make out her grandmother. G-Mom had the television on and the lights down low, the way she liked it when she watched her "stories." Even in the middle of the day, she preferred a dark room. Lucky for her, today she didn't need to worry about sunlight. It had been raining for three days already and Kuru expected more.

"G-Mom?" she called into the room. "You awake, G-Mom?"

G-Mom didn't answer. It was always a fifty-fifty guess if G-Mom heard her or not. G-Mom was seventy-two years old, half blind, half deaf, all rattlesnake. She lived in her chair and watched her stories, and the last thing Kuru wanted to do was to put herself in the middle of that combination.

But she had to tell her what was happening in the bakery.

"G-Mom, there's water coming in," Kuru said.

No answer.

"G-Mom? You hearing me? There's water coming under the door. You can see it coming right down the road."

"What water?" G-Mom asked, only half her attention, Kuru knew, swiveling to the problem. "Call the man."

"What man?"

"Mr. Perkins, that man. Don't let a little water fluster you, Kuru. We didn't raise you up to be flustered that way. . . ."

Then she went back to her stories.

Kuru had no earthly idea who the "man" was. Mr. Perkins, the landord? Taking a half step back, she wondered if G-Mom meant Mr. Pollywog, the lopsided man who went around town wearing overalls and the biggest pair of work boots anyone had ever seen. Was that the man? Were Mr. Pollywog and Mr. Perkins the same man? That didn't seem possible. She turned and looked at the water again. It had come under the lip of the door and puddled there. Out in the road, she knew, more water had come loose from somewhere.

She stuck her head back in the television room.

"You mean that man who wears the overalls?" she asked G-Mom.

"Yes, that's who I mean. He's the one who fixed the roof before, isn't he?"

"But it's not the roof, G-Mom. It's water coming under the door. Something's flooding."

The volume on the television went down to a tolerable level. Kuru leaned through the doorway, keeping her hands against the doorjamb so she could disappear if she needed to.

"Now tell me this again," G-Mom said. "I'm right in the middle of my story."

"I know, G-Mom, but there's water coming under the door."

Kuru pronounced the words like someone solving a clue on a television game show. All big, slow sounds so there could be no mistake.

"Under the door?" G-Mom asked. "I thought you said the roof."

"I never said the roof. You said the roof."

"I'm pretty sure Mr. Perkins fixed it last time."

"It's not the roof!" Kuru said, a little too loudly, she admitted, but she wished to heaven her grandmother would turn off the television and pay attention. "It's coming through the door is what I'm saying."

"That door is not going to let any water in," G-Mom said, pushing the button on the chair that slowly lifted her up into a standing position.

It took forever, as usual. Kuru waited and didn't say anything.

Finally, her grandmother stood on her own two feet.

"Show me," she said.

Kuru walked out into the bakery. It was afternoon, nearly dark with all the clouds. She didn't know how many inches of rain they had gotten, but it was plenty. When her mom left earlier in the day, she had commented on it. At that point it had just been an inconvenience. Now, though, Kuru suspected it was something else.

"Well now, look at that," G-Mom said, finally shuffling into the bakery. "It's flooding, isn't it?"

"That's what I was trying to tell you."

G-Mom nodded and kept shuffling straight across the room. She went to the front window and looked out. Kuru almost laughed to see her. G-Mom looked like an old turtle, or a chicken, turning her head this way and that, trying to get her eyes zoomed in on the water.

"Something must have broke," G-Mom said finally, pulling back as though nothing had been determined until she had witnessed the water herself.

"That's what I thought."

More water had come under the door even in the last few minutes, Kuru saw. She grabbed the broom from behind the cookie counter and tried to sweep the water out. But it did no good. If anything, more water followed the sweeps back inside.

"Give your mama a call and see what she says," G-Mom said. "I'll turn to the news."

"And miss your stories?" Kuru said, teasing her grandmother.

"That Illinois River is famous for flooding. You mark my word, that's what's happening."

"I'll call her . . ." Kuru said, then stopped when the electricity cut out.

It went out in one large *humppphhhh*. Then something made a loud cracking sound, the lights flashed for a second, and finally everything cut out again.

G-Mom turned slowly.

"Get the candles," she said when she had inched her way around.

Water, Kuru observed as she went behind the counter to search for the candles, had crossed the room almost as fast as her grandmother.

CHAPTER 2

I n the apartment above the bakery, Carmen Garcia, 12, rocked her baby brother to sleep. She sat next to the stove. Her baby brother had a habit of getting chest colds, and their mother, Eloise Clemente Garcia, had passed along this little trick. With the rain falling and the dampness in the air, the stove made sense. Her brother, Juan, took in the heat like a little sponge.

She didn't mind rocking her brother. Not really. Sometimes it was nice to sit quietly and do nothing except rock. It gave her an excuse to sit by the stove, and the truth was her brother generated heat like a hunk of lava. Or pumice. Or whatever the stones were that came out of a volcano. Anyway, he felt good in her arms.

She also liked watching her brother's eyes as they grew increasingly sleepy. It was like a game to make them shut and stay shut. Little by little, his brown eyes would close, then open, then close again. His breathing became quieter and his hands, usually moving to grab something, finally subsided. It wasn't fun in a big, enormous way, but it was still fun. Despite the objections she registered with her mother – *He's not my kid, Mama, he's yours. I don't see why I have to watch him* – she actually enjoyed the moments with him.

But when the electricity cut out she felt a little flutter in her gut. The red heat coils inside the stove slowly stopped glowing quite as red. The light over the stove switched off and something higher in the apartment building went out with a loud *pop*. She didn't move. For one thing, she didn't want to wake the baby who had finally dropped off to sleep. For another thing, she figured the electricity would jolt back on any second. It usually did.

So she kept rocking. After five minutes, when the baby was solidly asleep and the lights didn't return, she carried him slowly to the windows overlooking the street. It was nearly dark out and hard to see, but when she looked down she had a strange moment of dislocation.

Water in the street reflected the sky. Everything was upside down. The buildings, the street lamps, everything. She saw the moon sitting in the middle of the road.

Naturally, it wasn't the moon, not really, just a reflection, but it still threw her off. *Strange*, she thought. Yes, it had been raining and her mother had commented about a dam or something being under strain according to the news, but she had never seen the road outside the apartment building covered by water. Never. As she stood and looked out, she realized it wasn't just a skim of water, either.

It was a good six inches, if she could judge it from where she stood. It had already gone over the curb and ran along the sidewalks. She looked a little longer, then carried her baby brother to his crib and dipped him down into it. She kissed his forehead and tiptoed away.

She picked up her cell phone and called her mother. It took a dozen rings for her mother to answer.

"Hi, sweetheart," her mother said. "Everything okay?"

"The electricity went out, Mama."

"I worried it might. Parts of town are flooding. I heard it on the news."

"Are we going to be flooded?"

"We're closest to the river. How's the baby?"

"He's fine. I just put him down."

"It's early to put him down. Now he'll be awake when I get home."

He's your kid, Carmen wanted to say, but she choked it back.

"When are you going to be home, anyway?"

"Not for a couple hours, sweetheart. Sorry. I'm helping Mrs. Oldack with her group."

"Her book group?"

"Her other group. The knitters."

Her mother did maid work and sometimes cooked for rich ladies. Mrs. Oldack was one of her regular employers.

"Okay. I've got homework to do."

"I doubt there will be school tomorrow, sweetie. This

is a bad storm. They said it could get cold, too. The weather's gone crazy."

Carmen listened to someone running on the ceiling above her.

"The angels are bowling," Carmen said, which was a little code between them that meant the loud, obnoxious boys who lived above them were roughhousing again.

"Sorry, sweetie. Now I should go. I'll be home as soon as I can. Mrs. Oldack mentioned she might let me go early, but then she didn't come back to it."

"You should leave," Carmen said, then thought: *Because you have a baby.*

"We'll see. . . ."

Then her mother's voice shut off and the cell phone went dead and her little brother, as if on cue, decided that moment to wake up and start crying.

CHAPTER 3

In Apartment 3 at the top of the building – the building was only three stories tall – Day Johnson moved his body slowly around the corner of the kitchen, a green foam pool noodle in his right hand. He tried to spot his brother, Ellis, who had used the hundred-count to hide. The deal was simple: Ellis was a zombie, and Day was a hunter, and if Ellis could put his hands or mouth on his big brother before Day chopped off his head with the pool noodle, zombies won. Then Day had to become the zombie, and Ellis got to be the hunter – it was better to be the hunter, because you could smack the stuffing out of the zombie with the pool noodle – and the situations reversed. Day didn't like hiding as much as stalking. It didn't fit his personality, but, he admitted, hiding fit Ellis's personality like a glove. The kid was good at hiding. He was one sneaky zombie.

"You out here, zombie man?" Day asked.

He kept his back to the wall. He swiveled his head back and forth. Ellis could come out of anywhere, he was that good. And that quiet.

"Zombie want some brains?" Day asked, the pool noodle held up high so he could bring it down in a slash if he needed to use it. The rule was, if the zombie got hit by the noodle, he had to fall right away. Same went for the zombie attack: One touch of teeth and you had to lie on the floor and froth.

Day heard a pitter-patter of little zombie feet. He couldn't detect the direction, though. As he listened, he kept moving and his shoulder hit a colander suspended on the kitchen pegboard. The colander fell off and clattered to the floor.

"Zombie like? Zombie like noise?"

The thing was, Ellis was patient. Really patient. Day knew he himself rushed when he was a zombie, preferring the bold attack to sneaking. It made him nervous to be the hunter, but even more nervous to be the zombie.

"Come out, come out, wherever you are, zombie man," Day called into the apartment.

Then two things happened.

First the lights went. They simply blinked away. Day glanced at the street-side windows and he saw rain still falling, still blistering the panes. He opened his mouth to say something to his brother, but at that moment the second thing happened.

Ellis attacked. He rose up from under the kitchen table – *How had he hidden?* Day wondered – and came at him like crazed zombie. Starting so low, Ellis was toast. Day snapped the pool noodle down on his brother's neck, chopping off his head. To his brother's credit, he did a good job of dying. He fell to the floor and cockroached with his hands up, laughing as he did so. Usually Day would have lopped him again with the noodle, but the lights being out, the rain at the window, pulled his attention away.

"Hey," he said, "it's really raining."

"So?" Ellis asked, rising up to his knees.

"I'm just saying," Day said. "It's just kind of weird."

"This apartment is too small. There's nowhere to hide. Let's go down to the basement."

"Mom said stay here."

Ellis looked at him and raised his eyebrows. They didn't always do what their mom said.

"I'll be zombie," Ellis said. "You can still be the hunter."

"You just want to see the snakes," Day said.

"Of course I do," Ellis said, already starting for the door. "Let's go."

Kuru dropped the second five-pound bag of flour next to the door crack and then shoved it around with her feet until it connected to the first bag. The white sackcloth around the bag turned dark with moisture immediately. She supposed the flour did work in its way, but it wasn't going to work for long. That was clear.

"See?" G-Mom asked behind her.

"G-Mom –" Kuru started to point out how saturated the first bag had already become, and that the water still worked around it, then she closed her mouth.

Sometimes it was easier not to argue. She backed

away from the door and went to stand beside G-Mom, who had taken up a position near the cash register.

"Is the water still climbing?" G-Mom asked.

"Looks like it."

"Isn't this something?"

"I'll watch the store if you want to go back ..."

Kuru was going to say *go back and watch your stories*, but there was no electricity, therefore no stories. *Duh*, she told herself. It was easy to forget that simple fact.

"I bet something broke," G-Mom said, musing, her age-spotted hands resting like a pile of leaves on the glass cookie counter. "I bet some sort of dam or levee or holding place for water popped right open. It just stands to reason. Rain can't make this much of a difference in such a short time."

"It's been raining a long time, G-Mom."

"The police should come by. Or someone. Someone in authority to tell us what's what. I wish I had a transistor."

"What's a transistor, G-Mom?"

G-Mom slowly turned to examine her. She shook her head and used her tongue to wet her lips, as if they would need moisture to impart such learning.

"You don't know what a transistor is? Heaven, that's the limit. A transistor is a little radio, that's all. Least that's what we called them when we were girls. The smaller the transistor the better. They came from Japan, mostly. Oh, you weren't anyone unless you had a little transistor along with you."

"You mean radios?"

"Didn't I just say as much? Yes, transistor radios. Oh, gosh, they could be shaped like flowers or dogs. . . . My sister had one that was a sunflower face. It was the cutest thing."

"If you say so, G-Mom."

"And we only got AM on it. No FM in those days. Everyone listened to AM and you only got a few stations. Late at night sometimes you could get stations from far away. That was always exciting."

G-Mom didn't say anything else for a while after that. Then, as if settling on a plan, she said they should collect whatever candles they had around the place. Look for flashlights, too. Kuru looked in all the usual places: the junk drawer near the back door, the shelf above the bread box. She found a dozen candles, big ones, and two packets of birthday candles. She guessed there were more around, but it would take some looking to find them. She put them in front of G-Mom at the cash register.

"We'll save them until we need them," G-Mom said. "What's it look like out back?"

"Flooded."

"How flooded, though? That's why I asked."

Kuru shrugged, then walked to the back door and looked out. It was deep; deeper, probably, than the street out front. She wasn't great with directions, but the back of the house was closer to the river. Whatever was flooding probably came from that direction.

"Pretty high," she told G-Mom when she came back.

"Now, what in the world does that mean, girl? Pretty high? What if I told you I had a boy I wanted you to meet and I told you he was pretty cute? Would that satisfy you? Wouldn't you have a few more questions you might like answered?"

"I don't want to meet any boys, cute or otherwise."

"Oh, you're as stubborn as your mother was. But some boy will come along and that will be that. Now tell me, how deep was the water?"

"The dog house is floating."

"That rickety old thing? Should have been dragged out of here years ago."

"And the swings on the swing set. They're floating."

"'Cause they're made of wood. See? Now I have a solid idea of how much water we're dealing with."

"Ten inches, maybe."

"In back. In front maybe more like seven or eight, am I right?"

"You're right, G-Mom."

Before she could ask or say anything else, a siren went off. It was an old-sounding siren that went on and on and on. Something about the sound of it made Kuru feel lonely. She felt like the loneliest person in the world as long as the siren went on.

"That's an alert," G-Mom said. "You hear that, you stay alert."

"Alert for what?"

"Just a guess," G-Mom said, "but I'd say be alert for water."

CHAPTER 4

Carmen knocked gently on the bakery door. She knocked on the back door, where it connected to the center stairs, not the front door where it connected to the street. She kept her ear cocked to hear her baby brother, but so far he was being good. Her mother wouldn't be happy with her, knowing she had left her brother upstairs while she came downstairs, but it was getting dark in the apartment and she felt nervous and scared and uncertain of what to do.

So she knocked. And pretty soon the door opened.

Kuru answered. "Hey," she said, leaning her hip against the doorframe. "What's up?"

"I was just wondering if you knew what was going on. . . ." Carmen asked.

When the words came out of her mouth, they suddenly sounded silly. She looked at Kuru. Kuru managed to look bored. She wore big rubber boots that made her appear ready for anything. In contrast, Carmen felt like a wimp.

"It's flooding, I guess," Kuru said. "Not really sure."

"Is the whole town flooding?"

"My grandma thinks something broke. A levee or a lock or a dam or something. I guess it doesn't really matter what it was. It's water, that's all we know."

"I've just got my baby brother...."

"Oh, yeah," Kuru said.

"It's getting dark."

Kuru looked at her. Kuru was no one to trifle with, Carmen thought. She didn't take any nonsense from anyone, which was admirable, for sure. Carmen always felt soft around her, as if she had somehow let Kuru down. It was weird, really, because they were in the same class, but they ran in different crowds. Carmen was in student government; Kuru was a jock.

"Well, I just wanted to know if you knew anything," Carmen said, turning to go.

"You want to come in?"

"I have my little brother. . . ."

"You can get him and bring him down. We've got candles at least."

"I don't want to be a bother."

"I wouldn't have asked you if you were a bother," Kuru said. "Besides, the bakery's not going to get any more customers, I'm guessing, probably not for a couple days. We might as well close up and eat whatever isn't sold. There's plenty of food."

"Well . . ."

Carmen wondered why she hesitated. Why did people hesitate when they wanted to do something, but worried about inconveniencing someone else? She didn't want to be upstairs with the baby in the darkness, but she still hemmed and hawed about accepting the invitation. Her mother would have told her she was being a silly child and to take what fate had put under her nose.

"Okay, then," Carmen forced herself to say. "Let me just run up and get him."

"I'll leave the door open here. Just come on in."

"Thank you, Kuru. I was just getting . . ."

"No need to explain. This is a weird situation."

Carmen nodded. Then she turned and started back up the stairs. She had made it halfway up when she realized it was *dark*. Truly dark. The staircase ran up the center of the house so no secondary light came in from a window. Without electricity, it was simply a dark tunnel of steps leading up into greater darkness. It was actually a little eerie, Carmen decided. By blinking her eyes she could make figures appear out of the darkness. Of course they weren't real figures, just imaginary ones, and they had no more substance than creatures who lived under the bed, or in the closet, or in the bathtub.

The bathtub. Carmen didn't like thinking about the bathtub. As she continued climbing the stairs, she pictured the claw-footed bathtub in the tiled bathroom, the orange shower curtain tucked into the rim of the tub. *Why orange?* she had asked her mother repeatedly. *Why does it have to be orange?*

Because orange was not opaque, and it was not transparent, either. It was translucent, and Carmen could not pass by the bathroom, or even use the facilities, without feeling as though someone hid inside the tub.

Someone horrible. Someone whose movements began slowly . . . then gently, quietly, began pulling back the shower curtain. . . .

Carmen shook herself and forced herself to climb faster. It wasn't good to leave her little brother unattended. *The heck with the tub*, she told herself. *The heck with the orange shower curtain.*

But the second-story landing was dark. Way dark. *Impenetrably* dark, she told herself, using an English vocab word. The thing was, she realized, her apartment was not a whole heck of a lot lighter. She had to go down a dark hallway, push into a dark apartment, then cross the dark apartment and grab her little brother.

And she had to go past the bathroom.

And the orange shower curtain that sometimes breathed when she listened carefully.

Day smelled water as soon as he opened the door to the basement. The basement, he knew, ran under the entire apartment building. The building had three stories, three apartments, one basement, one center staircase. The basement, though, was something special.

He glanced at Ellis. Ellis pulled a face, laughing that it smelled down there. The basement never smelled that great to begin with, but this was worse.

"That's funky," Ellis said.

Day nodded. He still carried the pool noodle in his hand. He shoved it down the staircase a little, tapping the walls. The basement wasn't entirely dark. Some sort of emergency light had come on. Day couldn't tell what it was, but he guessed it was probably a light for the furnace. Or for the oil tanks or something. Something so that service people could find what they needed to find, even in a power outage.

It gave the basement a dark, terrible light.

"I bet they're out," Ellis said.

"What's out?"

"The snakes. They could probably swim right out of their cages with all the water."

"You're crazy."

"Teddy said they could swim. He's not lying. He said they could swim like demons. And the tops of those cages are just set there and they're made of wood, so they'll float up, I'm thinking."

Pythons, Day thought. His brother was saying the pythons were out.

"You're crazy," he said again, because he didn't think his brother was crazy. His brother was usually right about things like this. His brother listened to people, paid attention, made mental notes. His mother always read him the grocery list when they went food shopping, because he could commit that sort of thing to memory as easy as breathing.

"Let's go down and see," Ellis said. "We can just go halfway down and look."

"There's a lot of water down there."

"I can't see it."

"It's up to my waist, I bet. Maybe more."

"If it's over the tables, then I guarantee the snakes are out. Either that or they're dead."

"You go first," Day said, and snapped his brother with the pool noodle.

"You."

"You got to go down and check it out."

"We go together."

Day didn't like the setup, but he couldn't chicken out now. Besides, maybe it was worth knowing about the snakes. If they were out, he needed to contact the authorities or someone who could do something about it. If they were out, Teddy, the doofy snake farmer and cousin or nephew to the building owner, would be no use. He would pretend he didn't know a thing about them, even though he used the basement space to grow them and sell them on the black market. Burmese pythons, ball pythons, Day didn't know what all. Snakes as big as his arm. Yellow snakes, some of them, that lay in the light of the heat lamps with the hindquarters of a mouse or rat slowly walking its way down the serpent's throat.

"This is so bad," Ellis said, taking a step down to look.

"There's a lot of water."

"It's over the tables. Didn't I tell you? Those snakes are out."

He said "out" like OUT. Then he took a step back up toward the door.

"I am not going down there with those snakes float-ing around," Ellis said. "No way."

"Chicken much?"

"You go if you're so brave."

"Whoever goes down the most steps wins."

"Wins what?"

"The other guy has to call him King for the rest of the day."

"You're nuts."

Day took a step down. He turned and grinned at Ellis.

Ellis shrugged and took the same step down. "Big deal," he said.

Day took another step down. He figured there were maybe twelve steps, six of them covered in water. By bending forward, he could see more now. The heat lamps on the snake tables were out. Ellis was right about the water. It filled the basement about halfway, the level going above the card tables Teddy used for the snakes.

The tops to the cages had all been popped. The water had lifted them, or the snakes, sensing they might drown, forced their way. Day couldn't say for certain, but he was pretty sure the snakes were now swimming around in the basement, their noses up out of the water like speedboats.

"This is just nasty," Ellis said. "We got to let someone know."

"Who?"

"Teddy, for one."

"There's no way Teddy's going to cop to this. He'll pretend he doesn't know a thing about it."

"They could get out. *Out*, out, I mean. Out in the town."

Day shrugged. He had thought the same thing himself.

Then, before they could do anything else, they saw a snake. It came through the water toward them, its body swirling the water in a serpentine wake. It was one of the yellow ones, the ones that looked like a dead man's bones. Day shivered. He didn't like the look of it in a cage and he liked it that much less in the water.

"That is screwed up," Day said. "I mean, that's really weird."

"There's probably a dozen of them down here."

The snake came and lifted its body on one of the bottom steps, but it didn't slow down. It kept going, undulating right over it and continuing into the back of the staircase. Day heard another splash coming from one of the dark corners. It was weird, way weird. The water was bad enough, but the snakes made it completely freaky.

"Let's get out of here," Day said. "This is whacked."

"I told you they'd get out."

Day couldn't resist pushing the pool noodle down the last few steps and dunking the tip in the water. He waited, not sure what to expect. It only took a ten-count for a snake to slide by. It wasn't a yellow snake, but one of the big, thick-headed Burmese pythons. It seemed to size up the pool noodle, then sunk under the water and swam away.

Day backed up the stairs and shut the door solidly behind him.

CHAPTER 5

Carmen heard something yawn.

It wasn't a person. It was the building. It made a long, low sound like a ship going under the waves. *Like a movie ship, anyway*, she thought. She had never been on a genuine ship, so she couldn't say for certain what one sounded like, but it was the sound movie ships made when water finally came in and started to buckle the steel plate.

Like something needed to give. Like something *had* to give.

She heard the baby rustle in his sleep and he made a cooing sound as she stepped into the apartment. The cooing sound should have been soothing, a sign that all was well, except it was the sound he made sometimes when someone played with him.

When someone stood next to the crib.

No, no, no, no, she thought.

She started to tremble. She sent out a silent barb of annoyance toward her mom. *Where is she?* Obviously she had to work, but on a night like this, when things were going loopy, was it too much to ask that she drop everything and get home?

The yawn came again. So did the cooing sound.

"Juan?" she called into the darkness for her brother.

She waited in the doorway, listening. *This is not happening,* she thought. But it was. In the quiet she heard rain still hitting against the windows. It wasn't letting up. Nothing was letting up. The water would keep rising, she knew, and it had now entered the building somehow and put it under strain. She wasn't sure what kind of strain, but she doubted it was good. Maybe, she thought, the whole building could be knocked over. Didn't that happen? She had seen pictures like that on the news. The news always seemed like something that happened to other people, but for the first time in her life she realized it was also something that could happen to her.

She held her hands up in front of her and walked forward slowly.

And it went okay. She knew the apartment, where everything stood inside it, so she faced no worries about tripping. She kept her hands out and shuffled her feet just in case, and she made pretty good progress. She felt proud of herself. It wasn't the easiest thing she had ever done. She hummed a little song under her breath, trying to fill her head with sound, because the one thing she didn't have an answer for was the ...

... shower curtain.

I'm waiting, she imagined the shower curtain saying. *I'm right here.*

It was darker in the hallway. It was only a short hallway, fortunately, and her mother's bedroom was at the end of it, but before she came to the crib she had to go past the bathroom. She had to go past the bathtub, the orange shower curtain waiting like a lung slightly inflated, and she had to snatch up her little brother and head down to the bakery.

Her brother made a gentle laughing sound.

Like someone tickled him. Like he found something someone did amusing.

She stopped for a second and listened again.

Wind hit the side of the building. Something on the roof – it sounded like the roof anyway – made a grinding sound. Then, slowly, just underneath the other sounds, she thought she heard the metal rings on the shower curtain begin to push back. They slid. It was an eerie, light sound, one that would have been easy to miss in all the storm noise. It meant that whatever was behind the curtain had grown tired of staying there.

She ran. It wasn't the bravest thing that she had ever done, but being alone in a pitch-black apartment listening to the foreign noises of a storm can cause unnatural reactions. She ran forward and jumped like a deer past the bathroom door, and she did not turn her head left or right but kept it pointed forward. And because she was so intent on not giving in to her fear of the shower curtain, she forgot completely about the laundry basket alongside the wall near the entrance to her mother's bedroom.

She launched into the air going top speed, and the next thing she felt was her head piling into the wall, her neck snapping a little, and bright lights flashing behind her eyes. She did not have time for any more thought. Her world went shut and black, and the last thing she heard was Juan cooing from his crib and the leathery sound of the shower curtain fluttering in a breeze.

"You think they can get upstairs?" Ellis asked.

He was talking about the snakes. He couldn't get the image of the snakes out of his head. He especially couldn't get the image of the yellow snake down in the black waters of the basement out of his head.

"No, for the thousandth time, I don't."

"Teddy is going to go nuts when he finds out."

"I told you, Teddy won't claim the snakes. You won't see Teddy anywhere around here when the water goes down."

"How are they going to get them out of there?"

"How do I know? I'm no snake expert."

"I mean, if there's enough water, they can go anywhere. They could live through the summer, anyway."

"It's spring now, though. It's probably too cold for them. Your move."

Ellis tried to concentrate on the chessboard. It was hard to see the pieces in the candlelight. They had been playing chess a lot lately. Every day, maybe seven or eight games. Sometimes they played online against strangers when the Internet worked. Ellis was better at chess than his brother. Day played recklessly, while Ellis always played the percentages.

He moved his bishop to a spot where he could take his brother's knight. His brother could counter and take his bishop, but it would leave his pawns stacked. He couldn't move the knight without putting his king in check.

"I hate when you do that," Day said.

"Then don't leave your knight exposed."

Day advanced the pawn that would have covered his knight. Ellis took the knight, then watched the pawn take his own bishop.

"We should probably tell someone about the snakes, though," Ellis said.

The candle fluttered and sizzled. It gave off weird shadows.

"Who would we tell?" Day asked.

"I don't know. Someone."

"We can't call out. I checked and nothing's working. And I don't think anyone's coming by, do you?"

"We should tell Mom."

"If she makes it home, we can. But I think these roads are going to be closed off."

"So what happens then?"

"What happens when?"

"Like does the water just keep coming up?"

"I don't know. Not forever. Eventually, it will go down."

"It's weird. It's like you never really expect something like this to happen."

Day looked up. He shrugged.

"Eventually, someone will come by with a boat or something. They'll send helicopters, I guess. Something. You see it happen on the news all the time."

"What if the building tips over?"

Day put both hands to his throat and made a choking sound. Ellis laughed.

"I'm hungry," Ellis said.

"We can't cook anything."

"I'm still hungry."

"Maybe a peanut butter and jelly."

"I don't want that."

"Quit being a jerk and play. You can eat after the game."

Before he could make a move, Ellis heard someone knock. He slipped out of his chair and ran to the door. Day ran, too. They collided when they reached it. Ellis grabbed the doorknob, but Day karate-chopped his hand off it.

"Who is it?" he asked.

That was protocol when their mom wasn't home. Ellis should have remembered that. You didn't simply open doors to strangers.

"It's Kuru from downstairs. From the bakery."

Ellis looked at Day. He pursed his lips, then nodded and pulled open the door. The beam from Kuru's flashlight blinded him.

"Lower that, would you?" Day asked.

"We're eating a bunch of the bakery stuff if you want to come down. G-Mom sent me up to tell you."

"Thanks."

"It's just going to go stale otherwise."

"Sounds good."

"Have you seen the other girl? Carmen?"

"In Apartment Two? No, why?"

"She was supposed to come down and join us, but she didn't. I thought she might have decided to come up here with you."

Ellis looked at Day. He knew Day liked Kuru, or at least thought she was pretty. He talked about her sometimes.

"We'll just grab our stuff and come down," Day said.

"What stuff?" Kuru asked.

It was true, Ellis thought. They didn't have any stuff to bring.

"I guess we can just come along," Day said. "Thanks."

"Let's check apartment two on the way down, okay?"

Ellis grabbed the pool noodle from the kitchen table. It knocked over a few chess pieces as he pulled it away.

Knocking the pieces over reminded him to extinguish the candle before they left. He wet his fingers and doused the wick. Then, without really thinking about it, he stuck the candle and a pack of matches into his pocket. The wax felt a little warm, but it was okay. That was their stuff, he realized.

CHAPTER 6

You guys didn't have electricity, did you?" Kuru asked. "It may seem obvious to you, but I figured I should ask."

She had meant to ask that right off, but then forgot. It was strange to be with the two boys. They reminded her of dogs, of energetic dogs, who were kind of cute until they ran into your legs and knocked you down.

"No, it went out," Ellis said. "A couple hours ago now. Right before it got dark."

"Same in our place. Have you seen how much water there is?"

"I guess a lot," Day said. "It's still coming, right?"

"We're going to have to move out of the bakery. Out of the first floor. It's already knee-deep."

Kuru led them down the center staircase, flashing the light forward and back so they could see. She realized she had become so accustomed to the slowness of her G-Mom's movement that she almost couldn't believe how fast the boys traveled. Ellis, the younger one, jumped at the end of the first landing they came to. He swung himself around the newel-post and landed with a soft thud.

As soon as they reached the second floor, they heard the baby crying.

"He wasn't crying when I came up," Kuru said. "That's new."

"He sounds pretty upset," Day said.

Before either of them could say anything else, Ellis sprinted toward the apartment. Kuru watched, amazed. The kid just took off and went right into the apartment without knocking or yelling or anything else. A second later, Day ran after him.

"You guys . . ." she said.

Then she ran. She had no idea why she ran, but if they did, she did. She kept the flashlight beam on the floor in front of her. She entered the apartment, unsure of the layout. Then she heard Ellis calling from the back portion of the apartment. He sounded relieved.

"Got him," he called.

"The baby?" Kuru asked.

She felt confused. Why did they sprint like that? It felt like they knew something she didn't know, and that annoyed her. It annoyed her plenty. She stepped into the dark hallway – the layout, she realized, was not very different from theirs downstairs – and flashed her beam up and down.

It flashed on Carmen. It flashed on Day squatting next to Carmen, holding his palm against her forehead.

"You okay?" Kuru asked. "What happened?"

"I tripped on the stupid laundry basket, that's what happened. I could kill my mother right now."

Kuru went slowly down the hallway. Ellis popped out of the back room with the baby in his arms. He looked comfortable holding the baby. It was sexist to admit it, but it sort of surprised her.

"Why did you guys run?" she asked.

They didn't say anything, but they exchanged a look. It was a weird, knowing look. Kuru decided to let it go for the time being, but she marked it in her mental note-book just the same.

"I think I almost broke my neck," Carmen said. "I really do. When I hit the wall my head snapped back onto my shoulders. It's killing me."

"Your head or your neck?" Kuru asked, squatting next to Day.

"My neck, mostly."

Kuru used the flashlight to examine Carmen. She looked bad. She looked flushed and uncomfortable. Carmen held her hand on her neck and slowly moved in a circle, feeling for injuries. Before anybody could say anything else, the building shuddered. It rocked softly and made a *tick-tick-tick* sound, as if water had reached a new level. It was time to get G-Mom, Kuru knew. The water was rising faster than they could have guessed.

"You guys want to help me get my grandmother up here?" Kuru asked. "We planned to eat down there, but it's drier up here. You don't mind, do you, Carmen?"

"I don't mind."

"We may have to carry her up," Kuru said.

"I'll keep the baby," Ellis said. "Can you two do it? Why don't we put Carmen in a chair or something?"

That became the plan. Kuru helped Carmen into a chair next to the kitchen table. She guided her with the beam of the flashlight. Ellis sat on a chair beside Carmen and bounced the baby on his knee. The baby stunk, Kuru realized. He stunk like anything.

"We'll bring everything up," Kuru said. "Candles, food, whatever we've got. We might have to make a couple trips. First we have to get G-Mom."

"You got any glazed?" Ellis asked.

"I think so," Kuru said. "That your favorite?"

"I love glazed," Ellis said. "I really do."

He danced the baby on his knee.

"I don't know," Kuru said.

Day stood at the bottom of the steps, knee-deep in water, looking at the staircase in front of them. It wasn't going to be easy. G-Mom sat in a straight-backed chair, looking up the stairs herself with the flashlight beam. Sixteen steps, Day guessed. The staircase was narrow and steep, and he couldn't see how they were going to lift the chair with G-Mom and manage to keep it level. It was going to be heavy and awkward.

"We can't stay down here," G-Mom said. "I think I can climb it."

"I don't think so, G-Mom," Kuru said.

"Well, I doubt you two can lift me. Not up those stairs."

She had a point, Day acknowledged. But what else could they do? The downstairs was flooded. Water had come in everywhere and it now sloshed around in a dull, smelly mess. It was cold, too. Day couldn't say for sure, but he guessed the outdoor temperature was around fifty, maybe a little lower. With no heat in the apartment building, and with the water sapping whatever heat remained in the pipes, the temperature felt nippy.

"The thing is," Kuru said, "once we start lifting her, we won't have anywhere to put her down until we get to the top. I don't think we'll be able to rest her on anything."

"I can climb," G-Mom said, but Day noticed she didn't get out of the chair.

"Maybe if we get all four of us," Day suggested. "Maybe with four of us we can do it."

"I don't know if Carmen is going to be up for lifting anything," Kuru said.

"I'll run up and check."

He trotted up the stairs and found Carmen and Ellis at the table still. They had changed the baby, though. Day could smell the improvement. He explained the situation.

"If G-Mom will hold the baby, I'll help lift," Carmen said.

"With four of us it won't be bad," Day said.

He led them back down the stairs. G-Mom held her hands out for the baby without a word. Ellis handed him over.

"Once we start going, we have to go straight up," Kuru said. "One lift."

"We can do it," Day said.

And he thought they could. He took the front right chair leg. Ellis took the other front leg and the two girls took the back legs. They had to reach down into the water to grab the legs. On the count of three, they lifted.

Turned out, she wasn't heavy at all. Day nearly laughed. G-Mom was made of cotton. They went right up the stairs, G-Mom clutching the baby. Day told everyone to put her down when they got to the landing, but they probably could have kept going.

"That's the best ride I've had in years," G-Mom said. "Thank you all."

"Let's carry her right in," Kuru said, "then we can run down and get the doughnuts."

They whisked G-Mom into Carmen's apartment and parked her next to the kitchen table. She still held Juan on her lap. Ellis had set up a candle, Day saw. Otherwise the apartment was dark.

"We have more candles, too," Kuru said. "Downstairs."

"Bring everything you need," G-Mom said. "I don't want you going up and down with all that water around."

"I'll be okay, G-Mom."

"No, I mean it. You never know when this building may give a little. We got to keep to high ground."

"Maybe so, G-Mom."

"I'll go with you," Day told Kuru. "Ellis, why don't you come, too? More hands. We can make it in one trip, maybe."

Ellis stood. Carmen, Day observed, kept trying to get her neck working. It must have hurt like crazy to have her head snapped back like that, he thought. G-Mom had the baby standing on her lap. It was going to be okay, he decided. As long as nothing else happened, they were going to be okay.

PART TWO
SNAKES

SURVIVAL TIP #2

One of the hardest things to recognize in an emergency condition is that you have entered into an emergency condition. That may sound simplistic, or self-evident, but it is true. Our brains prefer the ordinary, the routine, and they will try to push for a return to familiar patterns. Accepting that you are in an emergency situation is the first step toward survival. Things will not return to normal immediately. Events have gone to a more extreme mode and it is in the best interests of all concerned to get that into the common conversation. The sooner one can grasp the reality of her or his situation, the better chance that person will have for survival.

CHAPTER 7

We should tell her," Ellis said.

They stood on the last three stairs of the center steps, watching the light beam move over the water on the first floor. The water looked ugly, Ellis thought. It was black and dirty and it smelled like gutters. Inside the water, under it, over it, all around it, the snakes patrolled. He knew that Day had promised the snakes would remain in the basement, but he didn't believe it for an instant.

"Tell me what?" Kuru asked.

"Oh, it's just a thing," Day said.

"Tell me," Kuru said, and she turned the flashlight beam on each of them, one at a time.

"You know Teddy?" Ellis asked.

"Teddy? That punk who thinks he's all street?"

"His uncle owns this building. I think it's his uncle, anyway," Day said. "So Teddy uses the basement."

"Uses it for what?"

"He had snakes down there," Ellis said. "Constrictors."

"Con . . . what?" Kuru asked, her voice rising.

"Constrictors," Ellis repeated. "Pythons, and red-tailed boas."

"Downstairs, below us?"

Ellis nodded. He saw Day nod, too.

"Let me get this straight," Kuru said, her posture growing rigid. "That idiot Teddy used the downstairs to raise snakes?"

"His uncle let him," Ellis said. "He made good money off it."

"I don't care what he made. How many?"

"Maybe a dozen," Day said. "I think a dozen."

"But they're in cages, surely."

"The water . . ." Ellis said, but Kuru stopped him short by pushing past him and going up a couple steps.

"You're telling me they could be down in this water?" Kuru asked, obviously freaked.

"They're probably still in the basement," Day said. "We shut the door. We have a key to it because sometimes we feed them for Teddy if he's not around."

"Feed them what?"

"Rats," Ellis said.

"Oh, it gets better and better," Kuru said. "Are you all out of your minds?"

"Lot of people think it's cool to have a python," Day said. "He makes good money off them. He really does. His uncle thought it was a free enterprise sort of thing."

"People like to watch them eat rats," Ellis said. "You know, certain guys do."

Ellis was aware that it all sounded a little weird when you said it right out. He liked the snakes, personally, but he supposed it wasn't a great idea to raise them in an apartment building. Snakes made good pets, actually. They were quiet, they didn't demand much, they didn't have to be walked like dogs, and they stayed where you put them, usually.

"Even if they were up here, and I don't think they are, they wouldn't attack us," Day said. "We're too big."

"But . . ." Kuru said, the light of understanding coming on in her eyes, "the baby would have been just right."

"That's why I ran," Ellis confessed. "Just in case."

"That is messed up," Kuru said. "That is so messed up."

"I'm telling you, we're making a mountain out of a molehill," Day said. "They can't get out of the basement."

"When was the last time you fed them?" Kuru asked.

"Oh, they can go a long time without eating," Ellis said. "That's one of the cool things about them. That's why they're good pets."

"You didn't answer the question," Kuru said.

"Teddy fed them last week for sure," Day said. "That's what I remember."

"Definitely last week," Ellis confirmed.

"Why anyone needs to bring a snake like that into this house," Kuru said, "is beyond me. I swear."

"If you don't want to go in the water, we'll go get the stuff," Ellis said. "Just tell us what to grab."

"You're going to wade through that water?" Kuru asked.

"It's not that big a deal," Day said.

Ellis hoped that was true. He didn't know for sure. There was one snake – Big Monte, Teddy called him – that Ellis wouldn't want to mess with. He was huge, for one thing, and he was nasty, for another. While the other snakes moved around the cage infrequently, and slowly when they did, Monte had more energy. He twined around the aquarium with grace and speed, and when they dropped a rat into the cage with him, he didn't hesitate. He struck and then rolled over the rat, squeezing it to death, usually consuming it before the others had even managed to kill their prey. Big Monte was a machine.

"I'll do it," Kuru said, coming down the stairs again. "I'll go with you. But I swear if I see a snake, I'm going to climb you guys like a tree. Do you understand me? I'm not playing about this."

"It's going to be fine," Day said.

Ellis stepped into the water. It came up to his waist, which meant it had come up a few inches even since they carried Kuru's grandma to the second floor. The water was cold, too. It was strange to think they were inside a building. You didn't think of water being in an apartment like this. He waited while the other two stepped off the stairs into the water, all of them feeling forward with their feet. Except for the flashlight, the apartment was dark. Ellis realized you usually counted on light from the street, or from the stars, for all he knew, but now everything was dark.

"So what are we getting?" Day asked.

"Just the leftover baked goods. And anything else we might need. We have some more candles and we need to get G-Mom's medicine."

"Why do you call her G-Mom, anyway?" Ellis asked, wading slowly after Kuru.

"Well, for a while she raised me. My mom had some issues. So my grandmother became my mom, sort of, and when my real mom came back I kind of had two moms. So G-Mom became short for my grandma mom."

"Makes sense," Day said.

"Let's turn in here," Kuru said. "This is the bakery."

The door wouldn't open. Kuru stood in front of it and turned the doorknob, but it wouldn't push inside.

"Maybe it's blocked," Kuru said. "I just closed it when we came out. I don't know why, really. Force of habit."

"The water has come up," Day said.

"This is weird," Ellis said. "Nobody's been by. We haven't heard anything."

"G-Mom's right about something breaking upstream. A levee or a lock or something. She says the Illinois River is famous for flooding."

"Let's all push on the door," Day said. "On three."

Ellis pushed and felt the door budge a little. He guessed something was behind it. Anything could have floated into position and blocked it. Of course, opening doors meant the snakes could move around more easily. He didn't want to mention that to Kuru.

They pushed again and the door opened enough to let them squeeze through. Kuru went first, then Day, then Ellis. The bakery was trashed. Water nearly covered the glass counters and it had lifted a bunch of free newspapers and floated them around. The newspapers swirled in the water like huge, white leaves in a spring flood.

"This is insane," Kuru said.

"Do you have insurance?" Day asked.

"How do I know if we have insurance?" Kuru asked, wading to the bakery counter and pulling out some

61

white waxed bags. "Even if people have insurance, it usually doesn't cover floods. Here now, hold these bags open and I'll put whatever stayed out of the water inside them."

Ellis watched her move around the counter area. She knew what was what. In no time she had filled six bags and three boxes with crullers, doughnuts, cookies, and three pear tarts. She handed them to Ellis and Day, then told them to hang on a second while she went into the bathroom to get G-Mom's pills. She sloshed away, the light disappearing as she went. Ellis stood in the water, in the darkness, waiting. He listened to the building, which groaned and popped. He knew water had pushed the building around, shook things that shouldn't have been shaken, twisted boards and nails and tried to bring everything down. He also heard the rain still falling on the roof.

He listened hard. And when Kuru screamed, it came as a surprise, a quick jolt of adrenaline passing through his body so fast it nearly made him drop his bags of baked goods into the water.

Δ   Δ   Δ

Upstairs, Carmen heard the scream. It didn't penetrate the walls easily and she only heard it as a distant noise, but she heard it. She glanced at G-Mom. G-Mom didn't hear it or she did a good job of ignoring it. G-Mom was cagey in ways Carmen couldn't quite define.

"You hear anything?" Carmen asked.

"Do I what?"

"Hear anything?"

G-Mom shook her head no. She still held the baby. Carmen was glad about that. Something was wrong inside her neck, and it was better, for the moment anyway, to let G-Mom tend the baby. Inside her neck it felt like a zipper had come off track, and now her neck was jammed or twisted in a painful way. It hurt more and more.

"Give me a second, okay?" Carmen asked.

"Where you going?"

"I just heard something from downstairs."

"They calling?"

"I don't think so. I'll be right back. You okay with the baby for a minute?"

G-Mom gave her a deadpan look. Carmen realized it was a silly question.

Carmen didn't like leaving the small candlelight of the table. At least, she reflected, she didn't have to worry about the orange shower curtain. Not with G-Mom around. G-Mom didn't play like that, Carmen understood. She wouldn't let things get out of hand.

Carmen had nearly reached the door when she felt a small lightning bolt flash in her brain. She didn't have any other word for it. She put her hand onto the doorframe and stood for a moment, not moving. The bolt came again. It was a brief flash, not truly painful, but disturbing in its intensity. It filled her mouth with the taste of metal and made her saliva run. Her right knee sagged a little. It made her dizzy, so she hung onto the wall until the sensation passed.

That was not cool, she thought as she regained her equilibrium. *Not cool at all.*

She rotated her neck and tried to get it back on track. It clicked when she moved. She didn't like that sensation.

She heard shouts downstairs. It wasn't a scream this time, just loud, urgent speaking at top volume. Carefully, she walked down the hallway, keeping her right hand on the wall to guide her. When she came to the top of the stairs, she paused. The steps went down into the darkness.

"You guys?" she called.

They didn't answer. Neither did they talk in a way that she could hear.

"You guys? Are you all right?"

No answer. She stood debating about what to do next. Part of her wanted to retreat back to the apartment, back to the baby and G-Mom. Another part of her pushed to go downstairs, to find the others, to help if they needed it. It wasn't as if she wanted to go downstairs. She hated thinking about the water, about the water climbing like a slow, ugly fog, but they were all in it together and fair was fair.

The lightning bolts decided it for her. A bright, heavy flash cracked inside her brain and she squinted at the pain. She felt dizzy, too. Her body convulsed. She tried to push away from the stairs, because she felt herself growing faint. Her neck made a series of angry, short jerks, as if the zipper had at last gone fully off its track, and she made herself back away so she wouldn't fall down a flight.

"G-Mom?" she called, but she wasn't one hundred percent sure her voice came through her mouth. Maybe she just called inside her head. Before she could analyze that sensation, she felt herself sliding down the wall. Her right knee gave out, folded like a shaky card table, and the lightning bolts inside her head flashed in a bright, quick sequence.

She fell down on the floor, her body limp and empty. The lightning bolt stuttered and frizzled, and she felt it pass up her body, up to her arms and fingers, then it turned around and roared back down the length of her body and shut down everything it touched.

CHAPTER 8

It was like a bad horror movie.

Kuru could not even believe what she saw.

She stood for a moment, her flashlight illuminating the bathroom, illuminating the mirror on the medicine cabinet, illuminating the thing she saw on the sill of the frosted window leading outdoors.

Oh, no, she thought. *Oh, no, no, no.*

She saw its reflection first. And that allowed her to tell herself that her mind had simply played a trick on her. She moved the mirror on the medicine cabinet slightly to get a better image of the thing on the windowsill.

The snake on the windowsill.

It had a cat in its mouth. A cat halfway down its mouth. Its jaws had flexed wide and now the snake simply slithered over the body of the cat.

She took in a deep breath.

Then she screamed.

She did not scream for effect, or to get anyone to come to her aid. She screamed because she had to. She screamed to let off steam, like a whistle, like anything that built up so much pressure that it had to release something or bust. She moved the mirror away, then back, then away again. She didn't want to turn and face the snake, because to do so would have made the snake real. Would have made the cat going down the snake's gullet real.

"Oh, no way!" Day said when he came flying into the bathroom, his voice a little too pleased and excited for Kuru's way of thinking. "No way!"

"That's a cat!" Ellis said, stating the obvious.

"Get it out of here," Kuru said. "Get it away from me."

"That's not so easy," Ellis said. "Why don't we just step away?"

"What's not so easy?"

"Just easier to move away," Day said.

He held out his hands for the medicine. She stacked the pill bottles on top of the cardboard box of tarts. She felt light-headed and shaky. She felt so light-headed, in fact, that it took her a long moment to realize a simple truth: *If one snake was out, others were out.*

"Anybody recognize the cat?" Ellis asked. "Did you have a cat, Kuru?"

"No, I hate cats."

"Probably a stray," Day said, his eyes fixed on the snake, Kuru saw. "Probably came in to get out of the water."

They like this, Kuru slowly realized. Both of the boys stared at the snake. She looked, too. It was pretty extraordinary, she granted. The snake had its eyes closed, or rolled back, or had membrane over them, and its jaw had unlinked top from bottom. It looked almost as if the cat deliberately ran down the length of the snake, but had become stuck and now moved in slow motion. The snake grinned as it ate. She understood that was probably her own projection onto the reptile, but she felt it was true anyway.

"Let's get out of here," Kuru said. "I can't stand looking at it."

"It's kind of beautiful, though," Ellis said, his voice dreamy and soft. "I mean, if you kind of take a step back, it's really kind of beautiful."

"You're a sick pup," Kuru said.

"They must be hungry," Day said, "to hunt so fast."

"Might have just been an opportunity," Ellis said. "Might have been too good to pass up."

"I'm out of here," Kuru said, giving one last look in the medicine cabinet to make sure she had everything her G-Mom would need.

But there are snakes in the water, she realized as she closed the door to the medicine cabinet. *You can leave, but the snakes might be out there,* she reminded herself.

"Let's go," Ellis said. "This water is making me cold."

Before any of them could move, the building made a loud, horrible groan. Something down below, down in the foundation, gave a shudder. Kuru grabbed the sink and held on for balance. As soon as the vibration stopped, she headed for the door.

△   △   △

Carmen wouldn't wake up. It was awkward, Day thought, because they stood in front of her, dripping from the water below, their arms full of baked goods, and Carmen lay stretched out against the wall, her body limp. Kuru was the only one who had the freedom of movement to bend down and touch Carmen. She put her hand to Carmen's throat, feeling for a pulse the way people did on TV, and Day realized he didn't have a clue how to assess someone's state of health in a realistic way.

"Why don't you put the baked stuff in the apartment, then we'll carry her back inside," Kuru said.

"You sure we should move her?" Ellis asked. "If she has a bad neck . . ."

"We can't leave her here," Kuru said. "This is no place for her."

"She helped us lift your grandmother," Day said. "She can't be that bad."

"You never know," Kuru said, her hand moving down to Carmen's wrist. "I've seen stuff in the training room when people get hurt in practice and you think they're okay, but they're not, it turns out. If it's a neck injury, it could be like an electric short. Something might have pinched a nerve or cut off some blood supply. I'm just guessing."

"Come on," Day said to his brother. "Let's put this stuff down."

"I'll keep the light," Kuru said. "Come right back. If I see a snake, I'm going to pass out."

"They're not aggressive that way," Ellis said. "Not unless they think they can eat you."

"That's reassuring."

Day smiled. It *was* pretty weird to think about the snakes being around. He followed Ellis down the hallway and turned into the apartment. G-Mom sat beside the table, the single candle flickering in front of her. She appeared witchy, Day thought, but maybe any older woman with gray hair would have looked that way. It was hard to say.

"Here's the stuff," Ellis said, sliding the waxed bags onto the table. "You okay, G-Mom?"

"I'm fine. The baby's fine. Where's Carmen? She went out and didn't come back. I called for her, but she didn't answer."

"She passed out in the hallway," Day said, adding his stuff to the pile of baked goods. "Your pills are here, too. And there are more candles. You might want to light some."

"We're going to get Carmen," Ellis said.

"Is she all right?"

"We don't know yet," Day said.

Day hurried back out with Ellis and found Kuru in the same position. She hadn't moved an inch. She had the flashlight pointed at Carmen's face.

"We need to be careful of her neck when we move her," Kuru said. "As careful as we can be."

"I'll take her feet," Day said. "Why don't you two take her upper body and try to stabilize it as much as possible?"

Kuru nodded and waited while Ellis came around beside her. She pointed the flashlight back and forth so everyone could see what he or she had to do. Then she clasped the flashlight in her mouth and made a grunting noise to indicate she was ready.

"On three, lift carefully," Day said.

He counted. They lifted Carmen and carried her slowly along the hallway. Day wasn't sure they really protected Carmen's neck as much as they should have. He tried to think of something they could have used as a stretcher, but his mind didn't come up with anything. Her bottom sagged in between the two points of suspension. He couldn't jerk her higher for fear of hurting her neck.

"Put her down for a second," he said. "My hands are slipping."

They put her down slowly. The next thing was to maneuver around the doorjamb and find a place for her in the apartment. Day told Ellis to go inside and find a place where they could put her. He came back a second later and said there was a couch near the table. He had dumped all the stuff off it, he said.

"Okay, let's go," Day said.

She felt heavier now. He had to spread his feet a little and force his hands to stay clutching her ankles. He told them to go through the door first and they did. When they came to the couch they lifted her higher for a second, then lowered her. Day had to readjust her feet once they had the upper portion of her body on the cushions. He doubted they had been particularly good at guarding her neck.

"What happened to her?" G-Mom asked.

"It's her neck, G-Mom," Kuru said. "Something's wrong with her neck."

"A young girl like that? My, my. Put a cover over her. Find something. It's getting colder."

"There's no heat in the building," Ellis said. "The boiler must be out."

"Why don't you go down in the basement and fix it?" Kuru asked.

Day smiled. He liked Kuru's sass.

Day watched G-Mom come over to inspect Carmen. She moved slowly, not particularly steady on her feet. She handed the baby to Ellis. Ellis took the baby and played with him. G-Mom told Kuru to shine the flashlight on Carmen's face, then she thumbed back Carmen's eyelids. Day couldn't say what that proved or demonstrated one way or the other, but G-Mom nodded.

"I studied nursing a long time ago," G-Mom said, letting the eyelids go, but still inspecting Carmen. "That girl is out cold."

"Is she going to be okay?" Kuru asked.

"Hard saying. She needs a doctor."

"We knew that, G-Mom," Kuru said.

"It's not good," G-Mom said, slowly standing straighter and moving away. "I know that much."

"What time is it, anyway?" Day suddenly asked. "Does anyone know? It feels like it's been dark for years."

"It's only a little past nine," Ellis said.

He held up his stupid pocket watch. It had a green face and could be set for an alarm, Day knew. It was a birthday present, sort of, a present he got when he took back two shirts their mom had given him for school. It had made their mom crazy that he would want a ridiculous watch more than a decent set of clothes, but she finally agreed it was his birthday and he could have what he wanted. At least it came in handy now.

"Is it still raining?" Kuru asked. "I can't hear anything."

"I think it stopped," G-Mom said, taking her seat again at the table. "I don't hear it anymore."

"That's something, anyway," Day said. "That's a help."

Then no one said anything for a little while. It was an awkward silence, one that meant an angel passed by, Day knew. That was the superstition anyway. If you looked at a clock when things went silent, it was usually ten of, or ten after, or twenty of, or twenty after. At least that's what Day had always heard.

They might have kept standing there forever if Ellis hadn't spoken.

"I'm starving," he said. "Can we eat?"

CHAPTER 9

We've got to get more organized about what we're doing," Kuru said, her elbows on the dining room table where they all sat. "Right now we're just reacting to things, but we've got to start planning."

"It's all just happening now," Ellis said. "Nobody could plan for something like this."

"Did I say we were supposed to be prepared for this craziness? I never said that. We're doing okay, given all the factors. But now we've got to get smart. We've got to think a couple steps ahead."

Ellis wanted another glazed doughnut. He had already eaten three, as far as he could track his intake. Maybe it was more. It didn't really matter, because there was plenty to spare, that was for sure, and it wasn't like they were going to stay fresh. Still, he didn't want to be a complete pig, even if they tasted amazing. He kept his eyes on the plate at the center of the table. The candlelight made the doughnuts seem to dance.

"Somebody will be by in the morning," G-Mom said, poking at one of the tarts. "You can count on that. When the sun comes up, it will be a whole different story."

"I'm not so sure," Day said, his upper lip flaked with cinnamon. "If this is a big flood, they might be a while getting to us."

"We got to get that girl some help," G-Mom said. "That's the top thing."

"Trouble is, we can't call out. We can't do much of anything except wait and try to keep ourselves safe," Kuru said. "But that's what I'm talking about. We should figure out how to have a water supply and how to keep it warm here. It's getting cold and we don't have any way to make it warmer. Things like that."

"And food," Day said. "We have the baked goods now, but we're going to need more if we're trapped here for a while."

"We should make an inventory. Examine the fridges and make an inventory," Ellis said. "And we need more flashlights. There must be some more flashlights in a building like this. It only makes sense."

Ellis still heard rain against the windows. It had stopped for a while, then started up again. It was a steady drone, not amounting to much; but added to the rain that had already fallen, it counted for a lot. He had never thought of rain, or water, as being powerful before. For him, rain had merely been a nuisance, something you had to avoid. Occasionally it canceled a soccer match, or a baseball game, but that was about the extent of it. The rain the past few days made him think his earlier belief in the world had been slightly naive.

It would be better in the daylight, he decided. Everything would be easier then.

"Maybe," he said, following the line of his thoughts, "we ought to just go to bed and wait for the morning. We're not going to die of starvation tonight. We can get around better tomorrow when there's daylight."

"That makes sense," G-Mom said. "That makes a lot of sense."

"We could risk getting hurt moving around in the darkness," Ellis continued. "Plus, I don't know, but there could be electric stuff."

"What do you mean, 'electric stuff'?" Kuru asked.

"If the water gets on the wires, it might not be good."

"He's right," Day said. "We should just sit tight."

"What about Carmen?" Kuru asked. "We let her just sit, too?"

"If you've got some sort of plan, I'll listen," Day said. "Otherwise, I vote we camp for the night and pick things up in the morning."

"We can go back up and sleep in our own beds," Ellis said. "We're on the top floor, so we shouldn't have a problem."

Ellis slid his hand forward and grabbed another doughnut.

And that's when he heard people calling for help.

"Do you hear that?" Kuru asked.

Because she heard it. Voices. People calling. The sounds mixed with the rain patter and it took a second or two to tease the sound out, but eventually she locked on to it.

"It's the wind," G-Mom said, turning her head to track the sound.

Kuru ignored her. G-Mom couldn't hear anything anyway.

"Maybe it's the police or a rescue team," Day said, standing. "Maybe it's help."

Kuru had a bad feeling. She wasn't sure why. It should have been a good thing to hear other people, but something about the noise filled her with dread. It was hard to say where the noise came from, for one thing. It swirled around and bent whenever it came close to her ears. She turned her head to try to follow it.

"Where's it coming from?" Ellis asked. "I can't tell where it's coming from."

"Me neither," Kuru said. "Everyone be quiet for a second."

She held up her hand to get them to be quiet, but just then the baby started fussing. Juan was hungry, Kuru knew. She stood and went to the refrigerator and looked inside for a bottle. She saw half a dozen lined up on the refrigerator door. That was another thing, she realized, as she plucked one out and carried it back to the table.

The baby was going to need food. They might be able to eat stale doughnuts, but the baby couldn't.

"Here," she said, and handed G-Mom the bottle. "Try to keep him quiet."

"The baby needs the bottle warmed," G-Mom said, but then she seemed to remember herself. The apartments had electric stoves.

Day sat back down. So did Kuru.

It felt like a séance, she reflected. It felt creepy and scary, with the white noise of the rain covering everything, and the distant calls echoing like sounds you would hear in a gym. The candles flickered and danced, and everyone's face looked a little carved. She felt if she could pinpoint the direction of the sounds, it would feel less creepy. But for the moment the voices might have been angels or devils, either one, calling to them all.

"I think it's upstairs," Day said finally. "It sounds like it's coming from the roof. You can hear it echoing down the staircase and through the heating vents."

"I agree," Ellis said.

"Is this building . . . ?" Kuru started to ask.

She was going to ask if this building was connected to the building next to it, but she knew that answer. It shared a roof with the Old French building. The Old French building was an abandoned factory building where The French Company made shoe polish back in the day. Kuru could see it now in her mind's eye. Yes, someone had come across the roof.

"Let's go," Kuru said. "G-Mom, you have the baby."

"Of course I do," G-Mom answered. "And I'll watch the girl."

"Carmen," Ellis said.

"Carmen," G-Mom agreed, tilting the bottle higher for Juan.

Kuru picked up the flashlight. It blinked when she turned it on. She slapped it down on her open palm.

"You guys have batteries upstairs?" she asked, inspecting the beam. It had grown softer, she saw.

"We might," Day said. "Mom hates buying batteries. She says it's like buying trash."

"She's right about that," G-Mom said. "Plastic bottles of water, too."

"You may be grateful for plastic bottles of water before this is over," Kuru said, bending to kiss her grandmother. "We'll be back as fast as we can, G-Mom."

"Just be careful," G-Mom said. "And just because someone wants to come in doesn't mean you have to let them in, you understand me?"

"Understood."

At least, Kuru thought as she led the boys out of the apartment, they were going away from the snakes. That was an improvement. In the hallway the sounds became more distinct. Definitely up rather than down, she decided.

"Up?" she asked the boys, just to include them in the decision.

Day nodded. Ellis grunted yes.

They went down the hallway and started up the stairs. The flashlight continued to blink and grow softer. She tapped it lightly on her palm, but that didn't improve things. It was going. Without the flashlight, it was going to be dark as anything.

"Yes or no on the batteries?" she asked the boys.

"Day?" Ellis asked.

"I don't know where we could find them. There could be some in the junk drawer. What size?"

"D-cells."

"Doubt it," Ellis said. "Doubt we have D-cells lying around."

"We're going to need light. Do you guys even know how to get up on the roof?"

"I know where the door is," Ellis said. "We'd have to hit an emergency bar."

"That's not going to ring," Day said.

"Sometimes they have backup batteries," Ellis said. "Like there should be lights in this staircase. There should be lights for an emergency."

"Everything is shorted out," Kuru said.

As she said it the flashlight died. The boys stopped on the stairs behind her. She tapped the flashlight on her palm three times, but nothing came of it.

CHAPTER 10

Carmen regained consciousness in dreamlike bursts. For a while she believed she was sleeping and dreaming, but it made no sense that she was on the couch. She knew she was on the couch, that much was clear, but nothing else fit into place. She felt a roaring pain in her neck and shoulders, a pain so large that it made her blink during the few times she managed to open her eyes fully. Her tongue felt fat in her mouth, as if it had swollen or had turned into a toad.

"Water, please," she whispered.

At least she *thought* she whispered. It was hard to know if the air that passed over her lips contained a word. Maybe it did, maybe it didn't. She said it again: "Water, please." This time she heard something move, but she couldn't figure out what it was. She couldn't really see anything anyway, because it was dark in the room and everything smelled of moisture and candles.

"You coming to?" G-Mom, Kuru's grandmother, asked, her face suddenly appearing like a cartoon moon upside down and above her. "Can you hear me?"

Carmen tried to nod, but that hurt at a whole different level.

"Yes," she whispered.

"That's good. That's real good, just stay now where you are. Don't try to move or do anything. You've suffered a fall. Looks like you twisted your neck somehow."

"Baby . . . ?" Carmen asked.

"The baby's fine, just fine. A sweet little boy. We've got everything under control, just relax. Just rest."

Carmen felt herself fade away then. When she woke again G-Mom had a bottle of water in her hand. She tilted it forward and Carmen drank. She had to think to swallow. It didn't come naturally. Her neck made a grinding sensation almost constantly. It felt like a model train she had once played with at her Uncle Danny's. When the train came off the track, and you only reset it onto three good wheels, the same thing happened. That was the image that came into her mind.

"Where is everyone?" she asked.

G-Mom gave her more water. Then she pulled the bottle back. The woman looked *strange*, Carmen thought. Her gray hair stuck out every which way and the light from the candles made her seem even older than she was in reality. If G-Mom had turned around and revealed an enormous turtle shell on her back, Carmen wouldn't have been surprised. G-Mom was a turtle, tall as a woman, walking on her hind legs.

"We heard some calling from upstairs," G-Mom said. "Seems maybe someone crossed over on the factory roof."

"The Old French place?"

"That's right. That's it exactly. The old shoe polish place. It's dilapidated, but maybe someone came up through it. Got chased up by the water."

"Is there a lot of water?"

"Halfway up the first floor by now."

Then Carmen flaked away. She jerked a little as she fell asleep and that woke her quickly, then she settled back into the cushions. She still felt mad at her mom.

Her mom should have been here, she reflected. She should have made her excuses and come home. Anyone could see it was an emergency. It was irresponsible on her part to remain at work under the circumstances.

But the rest of the thoughts fled from her and didn't reappear until she woke again. This time she woke to the sensation of something moving across her legs. It was a rough, scratchy feeling, like someone dragging a pine branch over her ankles. It passed quickly and when she opened her eyes she couldn't exactly make out what it had been. It looked like a snake, she thought, but that didn't make sense. They were in a second-story apartment in Illinois, not far from Interstate 80. Snakes didn't live in apartment buildings. Not big snakes like the one she saw anyway.

The next she knew, she heard people walking above her. It was faint and far away. Like the sound of reindeer, she thought, and smiled at the idea of it. Then she heard the feet coming down the stairs and she tried to keep herself awake, tried to stay conscious, but her eyes felt too heavy. She closed them and felt something sizzle inside her neck, but sleep conquered everything – rock, paper, sleep.

Day stood beside the door to the roof. He hadn't even known the door existed a few minutes before. He supposed if he thought about it, the idea of a door made sense. Maintenance people had to have a way to get out on the roof for repairs and so on, but he didn't have it fully in mind. Ellis did, though. Ellis knew the building better than anyone. His little brother was funny that way.

The door didn't have an emergency bar, though. That was unusual, Day figured. You needed an emergency bar for, well, emergencies. This door apparently wasn't up to code. It looked like a heavy door, but not the kind that should have been in place.

"Hello?" Kuru called, her hand cupping the candle that, luckily, Ellis had in his pocket when the flashlight went out. "We're trying to figure out how to open the door. It's locked."

"Hurry," a girl's voice came back. "Please hurry."

Day watched the candlelight move over the door, his eyes searching for a key or anything that might help open the door. With the flashlight they might have been able to find the key, but now that they were reduced to candlelight it was hard to see anything except the dull glow of light. He heard rain hitting against the roof. The candle glow passed over a fire ax. Day plucked it off the wall.

"I can open it this way," Day said. "I can chop through the door."

"Awesome," Ellis said.

"You boys are crazy."

"How else are we going to do it?"

Day watched Kuru think about it, then shrug.

"I guess a door more or less won't matter in this flood," she said, then raised her voice to call to the girl on the other side. "Stand back. We're going to chop the door down."

"Go ahead. Hurry, please," the girl's voice came back.

Kuru and Ellis stepped away. Day gripped the ax and squared himself in front of the door. Suddenly, the whole idea of chopping down the door seemed harder than he had considered. In the movies characters simply swung an ax and *bang*, the door splintered and broke apart. But now, standing in front of a real door with an ax in his hands, the door appeared much more substantial. He wasn't even sure it was wood, for one thing, and he wasn't sure he had much room to swing the ax. He didn't want to be a wimp in front of Kuru, but he suddenly felt shy.

He took a swing anyway. The ax made a terrifically loud sound but did little damage. He swung again. This time the ax head stuck in the door at eye level. It took him a second to wiggle it free. He swung again. The door sent out a couple chunks of wood. He swung again and felt sweat start to form on his chest and along his arms. It was work to chop down a door, he realized. Hard work.

He took six more swings, then handed the ax to Ellis.

"Be careful," he said. "Let the ax do the work."

"I'm a lumberjack," Ellis said, goofing around. "Timber!"

He only took three swings before he handed the ax to Kuru and took the candle from her. She did better. She worked smart. She swung the ax in a more precise arc, getting the head to hit into the door at about the same spot each time.

"Chop down at the bottom," the voice came from the other side. "We can crawl through."

Day took the ax back. It made sense to chop at the bottom. What was a hole at head level going to do? He stepped to the right and swung the ax like a hockey stick at the door. It was harder to get speed that way, but it was safer, too. He took a dozen swings, then handed it off to Ellis. Ellis was better with this method, but Kuru, when she took over, was by far the best. She chopped a small hole, then continued expanding it. Fresh air started moving into the stairwell. Rainwater came through, too.

Day made the final, explosive hit. A part of the door shattered and gradually it became easier to use his hands to yank out pieces of wood. Kuru worked beside him. In no time they had a hole the size of a steering wheel smashed through the door.

"That's big enough," the girl said from the other side. "Hold on. We'll come through."

Day stepped back, the ax at his side. Kuru lowered the candle so they would have light. A girl, a blonde, stuck her head through the door. She was maybe sixteen or seventeen and thin as a broom handle. She wore high black storm-trooper boots with the tops of her jeans tucked into them, and a black jacket with studs in the shape of stars punched into the fabric. As soon as she made it through she turned around and helped the creature after her. She didn't even look up or say anything.

The second creature was a pig. Day peered forward, trying to see clearly what he thought he saw. His mind didn't quite accept the evidence of his sight.

"It's a pig!" Ellis said, obviously delighted.

"What in the . . . ?" Kuru said.

The girl gradually pulled the pig through the door opening. The pig wasn't huge; it wore a rhinestone collar attached to a rhinestone leash. It was the size of a medium poodle, but much, much stockier. It made a snuffling sound as it squeezed through the opening. The girl held out her hand and the pig put its muzzle in her palm, snorting around for food.

"His full name is Zebra Moonface," the girl said, glancing up to look at them all, her voice high and thin and slightly southern, "and he's a Vietnamese pot-bellied pig. I call him Zebby."

PART THREE

SURVIVAL TIP #3

Canoeists — or anyone living near a river — should remember that the river they canoe today is connected to hundreds of streams and water sources above them. The river where you make your camp can be flooded within hours — or even minutes — by rains falling on streams and lakes many miles away. It is a mistake to see a river as anything but a snapshot of a moment in time, one that can be changed or altered by undetectable forces a day's journey upstream. Rivers borrow from all the waters above them and pass their cargo on to other water bodies below them.

CHAPTER 11

Kuru held the light closer to the girl's face.

"How did you end up on the roof?" she asked.

"And with a pig," Ellis inquired. "With Zebby."

The girl remained squatting next to the pig.

"It's a long story," she said. "A really long story."

"Let's take her downstairs," Day said, the ax still in his hands. "Are you hungry?"

"I'm starving."

"What's your name?" Kuru asked.

"Alice Wentworth."

"I'm Kuru. This is Day and Ellis. We're on the second floor."

"How high is it?" the girl asked.

"How high is what?"

"The second floor. The water's going higher. You can't believe how high the water is going to get."

"How do you know?" Day asked.

"Because I was out in it for one thing. The radio said it was going to be epic. They said anyone in the Illinois River valley needed to get to high ground."

"It's not going to go higher than a story," Ellis said. "It can't go higher than that."

"How tall is a story?" the girl – Alice, Kuru reminded herself – asked. "Ten, maybe twelve feet? It could go higher than that."

Nobody said anything after that. Ellis squatted next to Zebby.

"Can I pet him?" he asked.

"Sure," Alice said. "He likes to be rubbed around his ears."

Kuru watched Ellis tickle the pig. The pig had a permanent smile on his face, Kuru decided. He looked comical, actually, like a dog turned into a pig by a mean witch. But he seemed to accept Ellis's attentions without any problem.

"Can Zebby go down stairs?" Day asked.

"He doesn't like to, but he can. He's better at going up stairs. He's too heavy to carry."

"We should get back down to G-Mom," Kuru said, then saw the look of confusion on Alice's face and explained. "My grandma."

"Come on then, boy," Alice said, digging in her pockets. "I give him popcorn and dog kibbles. He likes the kibbles best. He'll do just about anything for them."

"It's only one flight of stairs, really," Day said.

Kuru made sure they had enough candlelight, but she had trouble concentrating on anything but the pig. It was a remarkable creature. Sometimes Alice dropped food on the step lower than the one Zebby occupied, and sometimes she led him with her cupped hand in front of his muzzle. The pig's short, stubby legs didn't work well on the stairs. He might have done better on a truly wide set of stairs, but the shallowness of the apartment stairs didn't give him room to rest his body. He had to have his front feet on the stair below him while his back feet stayed on the one above. Kuru sympathized with the animal. It wasn't easy being a pig, she guessed.

Little by little the pig made it down the stairs. Kuru wondered what her G-Mom would say at the appearance of a pig in the apartment. Under other circumstances, it would have been a funny meeting to watch. But given everything that had happened, she didn't imagine her G-Mom would be good-humored about it. G-Mom didn't love animals the way a lot of people did.

It took a while to get to the second floor. Kuru heard the baby crying when they reached the landing. She looked at Ellis, who simply nodded and went ahead. Kuru realized she would never hear a baby crying without thinking of snakes from that point forward.

"This is Alice, G-Mom," Kuru said when they finally reached the apartment. "She was up on the roof. And this is Zebby."

"Is that a pig?" G-Mom asked from the table with the baked goods set out on plates around her. "You're not bringing a pig in here."

"This is Zebra Moonface," Alice said. "You must be G-Mom."

"Zebra what?" G-Mom asked, and Kuru had to stifle a laugh.

"Zebra Moonface. But we call him Zebby."

"I don't care what you call him. A pig is a barnyard animal and belongs in a barnyard, not in a house. Take him out now."

"He's cute, G-Mom," Kuru said, although she wasn't entirely sure she believed the pig qualified as cute. "He'll be no trouble, I promise."

"A pig? In a house? I've lived too long, that's what," G-Mom said. "That's all there is to it. Your parents let you walk around with a pig on a leash like that?"

"Yes. They don't mind."

"Well, I mind," G-Mom said. "You think this is Noah's Ark?"

"It could be, G-Mom," Kuru said, figuring that might be one way around the pig problem. "You never know."

G-Mom, Kuru saw, pulled herself up to her judgment position. She kind of stacked her length on top of itself, building height along her spine. Usually G-Mom held forth on the government, or street life, or sometimes even a sports figure, but this time she didn't get a chance to proclaim anything before Ellis handed Zebby a doughnut. The pig ate it in one breath.

"Isn't that just the ugliest thing?" G-Mom said, clearly flabbergasted.

"That was awesome," Ellis said. "I want a pig when this is over."

"Why don't we all sit down and take a rest?" Day said. "It's going to be light pretty soon. Maybe you can tell us what you saw in the streets, Alice. And you said you were hungry, right? We've got plenty of pastries right here."

That worked. Kuru understood that her G-Mom would come to her senses when she realized a young girl was alone and, more importantly, hungry.

"Sit, sit, sit," G-Mom said, pushing a chair back for Alice. "Just keep that pig away from me. Filthy thing."

"He's not filthy," Alice said, slowly taking a seat. "He's a good pig."

"I don't care if he's the greatest pig that ever lived, he belongs outside."

"Out in the flood, G-Mom?" Day asked. "Come on, you don't want them to be outside, do you?"

"Not the girl. Just the pig."

Who knew how long they would have gone on, Kuru thought, except that Carmen interrupted them. Her voice came like a ghost's voice, slowly twining through the darkness beyond the table.

"Can I have some water, please?" Carmen asked.

"She's come awake," G-Mom said, as if remembering. "Bring her over some water, Ellis, and be quick. You sit down, Alice, and give us an update. This is the longest night I can remember in half a century."

"Who's got some water?" Ellis asked.

And that moment stretched out a long, long time, until Day said simply, "We're out of water. Clean water, anyway. Unless somebody has a supply that I haven't seen. All we have to drink is the floodwater."

"I'm in a band and I was driving to a gig and the water overtook us," Alice said.

Carmen listened to the girl's voice. She couldn't see her. She couldn't turn her head or lift her body from the couch, but her ears worked perfectly fine. It was sort of fun, actually, to listen to the voices going around the table without having to connect them to bodies. Her Uncle Elmer used to listen to radio-plays that he brought home from the library on old cassettes, and sometimes she couldn't avoid listening along if he babysat her. The voices going around the table reminded her of that, of radio shows with silly commercials for soap and cigarettes between acts. It felt reassuring to hear the voices.

"What kind of band do you play in?" Ellis asked.

"Grunge, sort of. We play all kinds of music, but mostly hard rock. We do a lot of covers."

Carmen heard Alice stop and bite into a doughnut. At least that's what she imagined Alice did. Periodic stops interrupted her story. Carmen heard boxes being pushed around the table.

"Don't worry about what kind of music she plays," G-Mom said. "Get back to the rising water. We need information."

"It came up suddenly. We were driving along near the river, not far from the train station, the old one, and next thing I knew we had to cross over a tiny stream. It wasn't really a stream, of course . . . it was a little moving water, that was all. But it looked like a stream, so I edged our car across it and it stalled out right away. I tried to get it started again, and as I was doing that I realized that the water was more than what I had first bargained for. Just in the time it took me to turn the key a couple times the water came up and started soaking through the crack in the door and in the floorboards. I have an old beater car, so I was used to that, but not used to so much water."

"What kind of car?" Ellis asked.

Carmen smiled. Ellis asked the questions she wanted to ask.

". . . give him the rest of the bottle," Carmen heard G-Mom tell someone about her brother. That was good. Her brother was in safe hands.

"An old Volkswagen Jetta. It's really junky."

"So what did you do next?" Kuru asked. "I've got him . . . he's taking the bottle. He's hungry enough, he doesn't mind if it's cold, I guess."

"I didn't do anything for a minute or two. I couldn't believe the scene right before my eyes. Water started flowing everywhere. I'm telling you, it was bizarre. And it was getting dark, so it was hard to see what was going on. A couple cars went past me and continued on, splashing me, but they didn't care. Big, SUV-type cars. Nobody stopped to see if I was all right or anything like that."

"What next?" Day asked.

"I gradually realized what was going on. At least some of it. The water kept coming higher and I worried that it was going to pick up the car and carry it away. But I also thought you should stay with your vehicle or something. . . . It was hard to think clearly. I mean, who's ever been in that kind of situation before? And I had Zebby here and he wasn't digging it at all."

"Zebra Moonface," Ellis said, and Carmen imagined him petting the pig.

"Eventually, I climbed out through the driver's window. The water pushed hard against me. Then I had to worry about Zebby. He was trapped, really, so I had to stay there and let the water get as high as the car window before he was forced to swim out. It was crazy. He could have drowned inside."

"No great loss to the world if that had happened," G-Mom said.

But there was a little humor inside G-Mom's voice, Carmen decided. A little levity, like she was having fun by complaining.

"Anyway . . . do you mind if I have another doughnut? Sorry, I'm really hungry."

"Go ahead," Day said. "So you were up to your waist in water?"

"We headed for the only building we could see, which was your street here, more or less. Zebby had to swim. Pigs can swim awfully well. He didn't mind the water once he was in it. A couple times I used him to pull me through."

"Zebby!" Ellis said, his voice filled with pleasure. "Hero pig."

"What did the authorities say?" G-Mom asked.

"I didn't hear much. I listen to music in the car, but I caught a little of the news. They said the river was up to historical levels, whatever that means. Setting a record, I guess. But from my experience, it looked like something busted and all the water came loose almost at once. It came up really fast."

"Why did you go up in the Old French building?" Kuru asked. "The abandoned building next to us?"

"It was the easiest way to get out of the water, that's all. I had to get to higher ground, because the water came right down the street. It was like a river, honestly."

"There's a limit to how high the water can go," Kuru said, apparently asking everyone at the table. "Right? I mean, it's not like we're in a canyon or something. The river valley just goes out into cornfields or something, doesn't it?"

"It's the amount of water all at once," Day said. "I think that's the issue. Eventually, it will whatchamacallit?"

"Disperse?" Ellis said.

"Yeah. Disperse. Right now, though, it's too much too fast."

"It has to be a dam," G-Mom said, "or a levee. I'm telling you. One of these locks they're always talking about gave way. Has to be something like that."

"I guess," Kuru said around a yawn, Carmen heard. "It doesn't really matter how it happened. The fact is it happened. Now we have to deal with it."

"We should get some sleep," Day said. "Everybody's tired."

"It's still raining," Ellis said. "It's raining harder than ever."

Then Carmen heard things wind down. A little later someone came over and stretched out near the couch on the rug. She heard other people making beds. G-Mom, assisted by Kuru, took a long time to maneuver into a recliner near the television. Carmen didn't feel particularly sleepy, but her eyes closed anyway. She heard Zebby make a low grunting sound. It was surprisingly soothing to hear it. If a pig felt safe, Carmen figured, they should probably feel safe, too.

CHAPTER 12

Ellis had made up a makeshift bed beside the kitchen window and the light that slashed in stirred him awake. Not that it was much light, Ellis thought as he opened his eyes and slowly sat up. Rain still pattered against the window, but at least the night darkness was gone. He looked around the apartment. It looked like a bomb had gone off with all the people sleeping in different postures and locations around the room. Still, he was glad that he and Day hadn't gone upstairs to sleep. It felt better to be around other people.

He tried to go back to sleep, but the baby fussed. He heard him gurgling and doing something and he got up to check on him. The snakes made him jumpy. The snakes and the idea of the baby – warm and bite-sized, oh, yeah! – made him even jumpier. He stood and tiptoed across the room, trying to be as quiet as possible. The baby lay on a blanket beside Kuru, not far from Carmen. He was wide-awake and playing with his hands punching up into the air.

"Hi, baby," Ellis whispered.

He bent down and picked up the baby. In that moment, something moved underneath the couch.

Instead of making him jump back in alarm, the sound cranked something way down in his gut. He stared at the couch skirt, wondering what he would find if he put his hand underneath it. Really, it didn't make sense to start seeing snakes everywhere, but something *did* seem to move when he reached for the baby. It might have been his imagination, or a trick of light, but he snatched the baby up quickly and walked him toward the kitchen and the growing morning light.

"That's a good baby," Ellis said, bouncing the baby a little. "You're a good boy."

He stood for a moment beside the window, surveying whatever he could see. The landscape had changed. That much was obvious. Everywhere he looked, he saw the reflection of water surfaces. Water had come directly down their street, but it also had gone up and into the buildings on the other side. If it was that high on those buildings, then it was that high on their building. That only made sense. Water sought its own level, which meant it would keep searching until the pressure on it to mount higher receded behind it. He was pretty sure that was true.

It was still raining. He had already seen that, but he noted it again.

"Hey," Alice said, sitting up.

She had made up a bed in the small kitchen. Zebby slept beside her. He made snorting sounds most of the night. Ellis liked the pig. He walked into the kitchen and sat on one of the small stools that Carmen's mother had arranged next to the counter. Apparently that was a place to sit and have coffee and watch the morning news. But there was no coffee this morning and no television for news.

"Whose baby is that again?" Alice asked.

Her movement brought Zebby awake. The pig climbed awkwardly to his feet. He was stiff, Ellis realized,

but he also had trouble gaining traction on the lino-
leum floor. He walked in a circle like a little old
man trying to loosen his bones. It was pretty fun to
watch.

"He's Carmen's mom's baby," Ellis said. "Carmen is
the one on the couch."

"With the bad neck. I got you. It was so dark last
night it was hard to see who was who."

"I'm Ellis and this is Juan."

"I knew you, Ellis. You're hard to forget."

She reached out and wiggled Juan's little foot.

"It's still raining," Ellis said, mostly to make
conversation.

"I heard it. That's not good. I wish it would stop."

"Someone should come by today. With a boat or
something, I mean."

"Maybe. Depends how many people are in need of
rescue. They'll probably try to figure out who needs it
most and then work around it that way."

"I guess that makes sense."

"But maybe they can give us supplies. We're going to
need water and food."

"I can't believe this is happening."

"Believe it," Alice said. Then she climbed out of bed and folded up her blankets.

Before she could do anything else, the building gave out an enormous groan and began to tilt. Ellis's eyes met Alice's. She held out her hands like a surfer getting her balance on a wave. The building gradually came to a stop. Everything inside – lamps, plates, pictures – chattered slowly as they skidded and came to new resting places.

"Whoa," Ellis said.

"It's the foundation," Alice said. "It's giving out."

"From the water?"

"Of course from the water."

The other people started talking. The building groan had shaken them awake. Ellis stepped over to see what they had to say. Kuru was already up on her feet, her head shaking.

"We have got to get going on a plan," she said. "We cannot be sitting around waiting for other people to rescue us."

"Easier said than done," Day said.

He sat up from his bedroll. G-Mom was the only one still asleep. *And maybe Carmen*, Ellis thought. He couldn't tell about Carmen.

"I want to go up to the roof," Kuru said. "I want to look around. Who's with me?"

"I'll go," Day said.

"I'll stay with Zebby," Alice said. "And I'll hold the baby, if you like."

Ellis handed Juan to Alice. He watched as Day picked up the fire ax.

"Bring some bowls and pans and things," Kuru said. "We can collect some rainwater at least."

"Good idea," Day said.

Ellis went through the cabinets and pulled out a big spaghetti pot and three Tupperware bowls. Kuru nodded and wrapped them in a sheet, then tossed them over her shoulder.

"We'll be back," she said. "Let G-Mom sleep as long as she likes. She's easier to handle when she's asleep."

"We've got to scavenge everything we can while there's light," Kuru said into the mini-huddle they had formed in the hallway just outside the door. "We should go to your apartment after we visit the roof. Look in the fridge, check for canned foods. You know, everything. There's hardly anything in Carmen's apartment."

Day nodded. Kuru was impressive. She possessed a steady, calm manner that instilled confidence. In fact, the only thing that threw her off was the appearance of the snakes. Otherwise, she was boss.

After speaking, she turned and hustled up the stairs. Day followed. Ellis brought up the rear. They made much better time now without the pig and in adequate light. Day felt a small bubble of optimism enter his thinking. It was okay. It was going to be a mess, but at least, he reflected, their apartment hadn't been affected. The water couldn't reach that high.

At the door to the roof, he scrambled through the opening on his hands and knees, pushing the ax in front of him. Kuru chucked the pan and the bowls through. In a flash they made it outside. The wind felt fresh and good.

"Wow," Kuru said, looking around. "Holy mackerel."

Day looked around, too. Water everywhere. *Everywhere!* Swiveling his head in a slow circle, he took it all in. For some reason, it reminded him of a sand castle he had once built on a sandbar in Lake Michigan. Little by little, the tide came in and covered the sand castle. On a lake the tides weren't that great, but the water did slowly rise and touch the front of the castle, caving it in. That's what the town looked like now. Water had taken everything and turned it dark and ugly. Maybe it wasn't a sand castle, he decided. Maybe it was a big, wet rag that was so saturated it couldn't budge without letting more water free. He had never seen anything like it.

"Amazing," Ellis said.

"This is not good," Kuru said. "Not good at all."

"Is that the post office?" Ellis asked, pointing southwest.

"I think so. And that's the clock tower. School's over there," Day said, beginning to pick up landmarks.

"It's all underwater," Kuru said, walking around the roof to get a better look. "And nothing's moving. I don't see anyone, do you all?"

"No one," Ellis agreed.

"Not anything," Kuru said. "That's weird. You would think something would be out, looking around. A boat or something. No helicopters, either."

Day did see something. He squinted to see better, then pulled back as though he'd been hit. Horses. Drowned horses. Three of them, he saw, bobbing in the water like swollen islands. He didn't want to think too hard about the horses struggling, or about other creatures that might have been trapped by the floodwaters.

"Let's set out the bowls," Ellis said. "And we should make a sign or something that lets people know we're here."

"Good idea," Kuru said, starting to untie the bowls and pot from the sheet. "We can write something on the sheet. Make a flag or something."

"Doesn't look like anyone's coming," Day said.

"Hard to know what's happening," Kuru said. "The airports could be flooded. Rescue teams, you never know. They may be trying, but they can't get out to assist anyone. It's better to concentrate on what we can

control and not worry about who is doing what somewhere else."

Day nodded. He agreed. He took the spaghetti pot
when Kuru handed it to him and studied it for a moment.

"We should get something to funnel more water in,"
he said. "Like a shower curtain or something."

"Good idea. You want to run down and get one?"

"Okay."

"Bring up more containers," Kuru said. "Looks like
we're going to be here awhile."

"And a marker," Ellis said. "The big one Mom got.
It's in the bowl in the kitchen . . . you know."

"Anything else?"

"Not right now. Maybe later."

"I'll be right back."

"Take your time. There's no rush. Be careful, because
anyone gets injured and they're out of luck," Kuru said.
"Just think of Carmen."

"I'll be careful."

"Man, I wish it would stop raining," Ellis said. "It's
getting me down."

Day climbed back through the hole in the door. He paused, wondering if he should take a minute to search for a key or smash it open wider, but decided it didn't matter. G-Mom wasn't going to come up on the roof anytime soon, and anyone else from the group could crawl through. He zipped down the stairs and followed the third-floor hallway to his apartment. He pushed open the door and for a second, just a second, a sense of normalcy covered him. It might have been any day, no big deal – the apartment waiting patiently, food in the fridge, his mom due home in an hour or two. He knew what he would do if it was a normal day: an hour of video games, maybe against Ellis, then homework, then chess while they began cooking dinner. As he stood in the kitchen, looking around, that suddenly seemed like the greatest day anyone could have. He wondered why he had never noticed it before. You had to lose something to gain something, he realized.

He went through the refrigerator. There wasn't much, but he did find some milk that he could bring to the baby. He set it on the kitchen counter. Then he made a pile of some Swiss cheese; some ham slices that didn't look great; a browned head of lettuce; strawberry jelly; three-quarters of a pound of butter; a half dozen eggs, hard-boiled or not, he wasn't sure; a half-empty can of spray whipped topping; a jar of sandwich sweet-and-sour pickles; a can of Diet 7-Up; and a sleeve of white crackers. He left it on the counter while he went back into the apartment and pulled the shower curtain off its rings. It made a crackling noise with its stiffness, and it wasn't easy to fold, but eventually he got it small enough to carry in front of him like an armful of blankets. Passing back into the kitchen, he decided not to bother with the food for the time being. They could get it later. He found the black marker in the bowl where Ellis said it would be, jabbed it into his hip pocket, then looked around to see what he might have forgotten.

His eyes passed over the snake without seeing it.

Or rather, he *saw* it, but he didn't register it. It was like one of those perception problems you sometimes got in school – which object does not belong? – and his eyes slid right over the snake and onto the two ancient bananas his mother had hung from the banana holder thing.

Day backed his eyes up. Once he finally picked out the snake, it was impossible to see anything else.

"Hey," he said to no one. He moved the shower curtain a little more carefully in front of him.

The snake wasn't hissing or aggressive. It lay like a rope across the kitchen counter, not far from the stove, its head secured on the bread board, but the rest of its body draped casually downward across the face of the cupboards. Day didn't freak. He didn't love snakes, it was true, but he also didn't fear them. Ellis loved them, and so did Teddy in a sort of gruff, professional way, but Day simply respected them. They were creatures, somewhat valuable creatures, and he didn't mind picking up a few extra dollars taking care of them when Teddy wasn't around. But taking care of them while they rested under a heat lamp in a wired aquarium was one thing. Standing in front of one, eye to eye, so to speak, was a different equation altogether.

He wondered how long it had been watching him. He wondered how he could have missed it.

Day moved in a careful semicircle away from the snake. He kept the shower curtain in front of him the entire time. When he made it to the door, he trotted to the stairs, then bolted up them. The snake had given him the willies. Even if it had attacked, which was unlikely, he probably would have been okay. He could have carried the snake upstairs and called for Ellis and Kuru.

Still, the snake had triggered a primitive shiver down in his brain stem and he ran up the stairs, feeling like a lion chased him. It was almost funny. He jammed through the door, shoving the shower curtain ahead of him, then scrambled out onto the roof.

"I saw one," Day said as soon as he came to a rest beside them. "A snake. A red-tailed boa."

"Where?" Ellis asked.

"In our apartment. On the counter."

"That means they're everywhere," Ellis said. "That means they could be anyplace."

"I hate you both so much right now," Kuru said. "I hope you know that."

"We should tell the others," Day said.

"G-Mom is going to freak," Kuru said, emphasizing each word. "Pigs and snakes. She will not be happy."

"I thought I saw one under the couch when I picked up the baby this morning," Ellis said. "I couldn't be sure, but I thought so."

"We should get down there fast," Day said. "They're probably hungry."

"How do you find them?" Kuru asked, taking the shower curtain and spreading it out. She propped part of it on a ventilation shaft, then tucked the plastic into a funnel-ramp that ended in the spaghetti pot.

"Teddy told us if a snake went missing," Ellis said, "you should check any place where they can hide. In backpacks, in seat cushions, under a bookcase, anywhere. They depend on hiding, then ambushing their prey."

"You think Zebby is too big for them?" Day asked. "I think he might be."

"Not too big for Big Monte," Ellis said. "Big Monte could take him down."

"Who is Big Monte?" Kuru asked. "I don't really want to know, but I feel that I should."

"He's the meanest snake Teddy ever raised," Day said. "And the biggest."

"Teddy sold him to a guy and the guy brought him back because he was afraid of him. This was a tough guy, too," Ellis said, "so it was a big deal for him to admit he was afraid of a snake. He had to have three people hold the snake if he wanted to move him."

"Big Monte could eat Zebby for sure," Day said. "I'd bet on it."

Before they could say anything, they heard a scream from inside the building. It went on a long, long time, and it was so filled with terror there was no mistaking what it was. Day ran toward the door and snatched up the ax as he went. He heard Ellis and Kuru scrabbling after him.

CHAPTER 13

Carmen heard the pig get hit.

It sounded dull and thick, like someone swatting a carpet hanging on a line with the end of a baseball bat. *Thunk*. Or *thud*. Then she heard something whisper, something slithery and quick, and the next thing she knew she heard the pig let out a squeal. It was amazingly loud. It filled the apartment and threatened to break the windows for all Carmen could tell. Inside the sound, though, she heard the scaly crawl of the snake, its strength pushing something aside, the leg of a chair or something, and Carmen's own mouth opened to scream beside all the other noise, but her neck went into spasm and wouldn't let her emit a sound.

Then things became even crazier. She heard yelling and running and G-Mom's voice came over everything. G-Mom screamed, but it wasn't a 'fraidy-cat scream, but a battle cry instead, and she watched as G-Mom tottered forward with a standing lamp. She jabbed the lamp base at the bundle of snake and pig, and the pig responded with more squealing and the snake continued roiling around the pig, finding him with all of its body.

"Get off him, get off him!" the girl in black boots shouted, and she kicked at the fighting animals. "Get off him!"

"Pull at his head," G-Mom said. "He's got his bite in him."

Pandemonium. Another lamp went over. The pig struggled and tried to run, but the snake weighed too much. Nevertheless, he managed to run a little ways with the snake around him like a pool float tube. She didn't know if she imagined it, but she seemed to hear the pig wheezing. He was losing his breath, she thought, and she wasn't sure why that was happening.

"Oh, you evil, evil thing!" G-Mom yelled. "You leave that animal alone!"

Then, like superheroes, Kuru and Ellis and Day arrived. They flashed into the apartment, and Carmen watched as Ellis fell on the pig and snake and worked his hand behind the snake's head. He said something about it not being Big Monte, whatever that meant, and he cursed once while he tried to wrestle the serpent's head free from the pig. Day seemed to know what to do, too, because he began unwinding the snake, removing it loop by loop from the pig's torso. The pig now lay still as if in shock.

"Grab him and pull him away!" Ellis said to the new girl. "Peel him off Zebby."

"I don't want to touch him!" the girl said.

"Well, if you don't Zebby's going to die."

That persuaded the girl, Carmen saw. She hooked her hands around the belly of the snake, while Kuru took what would have been the shoulders on any other animal. Little by little they uncurled the snake, extending it to its full length. It still tried to tuck and pull together. It nearly jerked the new girl off her feet a couple times.

Zebby did not move, but he seemed to be breathing, Carmen saw.

"What are we going to do with him?" Ellis asked from the head. "The cages are all downstairs."

He held the head carefully away from his body. Carmen couldn't tell who he addressed, but Day answered.

"We'll take him upstairs and throw him off the roof."

"Are you crazy?" Ellis asked, struggling to maintain control of the head.

"What else are we going to do with him?"

"Chop him in half," G-Mom said. "Just get rid of him."

Then they made a few communicating motions apparently, because the next thing Carmen knew they started carrying the snake toward the door. It forced them to back up twice and thread the needle of the doorway because its strength kept throwing them off. It was a spectacle to see them weave out, the snake connecting them like a diamond-studded rope.

"What are we going to do with him?" Kuru asked, her breath rasping and thin.

They stood in the hallway, the snake stretched out between them. The snake continued to move and twist, and Kuru couldn't believe its strength. It had attacked the pig, wrestled it, and now it twisted and fought against its own capture. Like it or not, it was an amazing creature. Nevertheless, the simple fact was they had no place to put the snake. They couldn't hold it forever.

"There's a storage closet at the end of the hall," Day said. "We can stick him in there."

"They have really sharp teeth," Ellis said, "and the teeth point backward so it's hard to get them out if they bite you. We've got to be careful when we let him go."

Kuru had every intention of being careful. She walked down the hallway, holding the snake against her body to still it. Alice walked in front of her. Day led them to the storage closet and paused. It wasn't going to be easy, Kuru saw, to get the snake inside, release it without getting bitten, then close the door on it.

"How do you want to do this?" Alice asked.

"The trick is to let it all go at once," Ellis said. "If I let go of the head first, it might bite one of us."

"Let me open the door," Day said, "and see how big it is inside. Hold the snake tight."

He kept one hand on the snake and used the other to open the door to the storage closet. Kuru saw the closet looked to be in rough shape. The shelves it had once had on the wall had fallen off and stood like jackstraws in a tangled mess. The drywall wasn't in good shape, either. Hunks of it had pried off the wall, and Kuru wondered if putting the snake inside would only make them feel like they had done something. The snake might be able to get out through the holes in the wall. It was impossible to know what a snake could do under these circumstances.

"We could kind of throw the snake inside," Ellis said, his eyes studying the closet. "Just swing it in and let it go on the count of three. Then I would have the head, and I could throw it last."

"You're the boss," Alice said.

"It's going to want to bite something," Day said. "That's all it knows how to do. It will bite and hold on. We need it to retreat."

"Let's try it," Ellis said. "We can always unwind it again and start all over."

It was awkward, Kuru reflected. They couldn't all fit through the doorway to the storage closet at once or in a coordinated way. One person had to let go of the snake, then the next, and so on. Ellis came up with another suggestion.

"I'm going to put the head down first," he said. "I'll put it inside the closet and maybe the snake will just crawl away."

"What if it tries to bite us?" Alice asked.

"Then we're in trouble. But I don't think it will. It's scared and tired. It may just want to get away."

"This is crazy," Kuru said, because it was. It felt crazy.

"Let's try it," Ellis said. "Ready? I'm going to lower its head to the ground and you all let the body go one by one. Be gentle. You don't want to corner it or make it feel threatened."

Ellis didn't wait for an argument or further discussion. He put the snake's head on the inside of the storage closet. The snake didn't try to bite or do anything except slither away. Kuru dropped her portion of the snake, then Alice, and finally Day. Ellis had to butt the door against the last portion of the snake. Then, with a final flip of its tail, the snake disappeared behind the door into the closet.

Ellis high-fived his brother. Then they all high-fived. It felt good, Kuru realized, to work as a team.

"That was intense," Alice said, her color bright. "That was wicked intense."

"You need one person per four feet of snake," Ellis said. "According to Teddy. They can kill you inside of two minutes."

"I've got to go check on Zebby," Alice said, as if suddenly remembering. "What a nightmare for him."

Maybe it was the mention of Zebby, or the solid sensation of having a door between her and the snake, but Kuru's mind suddenly cleared.

"Where was the baby?" she asked. "When we went in to help, I didn't see the baby."

"I put him in his crib . . ." Alice began, but didn't finish.

They ran. Kuru ran the fastest, but they all ran.

Δ   Δ   Δ

Kuru stopped so suddenly, Ellis couldn't help piling into her. She braced herself in the doorway, staring. Ellis heard the baby make a fussing sound. Day skidded to a stop behind him. Then Alice.

Ellis saw the baby in G-Mom's arms. The baby was fine.

"What?" G-Mom said, evidently reading the alarm on their faces.

"We just worried . . ." Kuru started to explain.

"I know what you children were worried about," G-Mom said, her voice raising to a scolding level. "But I've got the baby right here. Right in my arms. Now I want you to get in here and tell me every last thing about these snakes. I'm so angry right now I could pop a vein. I surely could. Who is responsible for these snakes being in this apartment building? Is it one of you boys? Step in here and tell me straight. We only fear what we don't know."

Ellis wanted to curl away and head for the roof, but Alice pushed past him and went to Zebby. The pig no longer rested on his side, but he wasn't on his feet, either.

He appeared stunned and confused. Alice reached in her pocket and gave him some kibbles. He barely bothered with them.

"It may have broken his ribs," Ellis said, the words coming out before he had fully considered their impact. "I don't mean to bum you out, but they're really strong. The snakes, I mean."

"All his ribs?" Alice asked, her voice turning into a cry.

"No, probably not," Ellis said hurriedly. "Probably not all his ribs. But maybe one or two, or maybe they're just bruised. It's hard to say. He'll probably get better soon."

Ellis looked over at G-Mom. She pointed to a chair by the table. Ellis nodded and sat down. Ellis caught Day's eye and told him, with a nod, to join him. But Day made an excuse.

"I left some food out on the counter," he said, "up in our apartment. Kuru, will you come with me? We can check the water, too."

"Okay."

"Ellis knows the snakes better than anyone," Day said.

"Then we're going to have a little conversation," G-Mom said. "Sit up straight and talk to me."

Ellis watched Kuru and Day duck out and head for the third floor. He hated them a little in that moment, because they were free and he wasn't. He took a deep breath and told G-Mom what he knew about the snakes once she settled down across from him at the table. She asked a lot of questions. Alice, petting Zebby, asked a couple, too. Mostly they wanted to know how many there were, what they ate, who was behind it all. Ellis told them what he knew, shielding them from the gorier details. Like the rabbit feedings. Like the rats.

"That boy Teddy sold these snakes?" G-Mom asked when Ellis concluded his retelling of the events. "Who would buy such a thing?"

"Some people like them, G-Mom. Some people think they're really cool. You know how kids buy pit bulls and turn them nasty? Same idea."

"You mean those ugly dogs you see around?"

Ellis nodded. He actually liked pit bulls, but not when they were trained to be vicious. Alice came over and sat down with him. Ellis ate one of the last doughnuts. He felt empty inside. Not hungry, really, just empty. He asked if he could hold the baby. He liked holding Juan. It made him feel less empty.

"How do we keep them out?" Alice asked. "The snakes, I mean."

"Keep the door closed. We should all be alert, and we should keep the baby with us at all times. We should never put him down. Not until this is over. And we should travel in pairs at least."

"But we still don't know how many might be creeping around this building, do we?" G-Mom asked.

Ellis bounced the baby a little. He shook his head. "Not exactly. I think six or so."

"I've lived too long," G-Mom said, shaking her head. "I really mean it."

"Mostly the snakes just lay there and don't do much of anything," Ellis said, feeling a need to defend them a little. "They bask in the heat lamp and eat once a week or so. They're nice pets. All of them are domestic snakes except one. Only one was wild-captured."

"What's that mean?" Alice asked.

Ellis realized he had gone too far, but he decided to make a clean break of it.

"Domestic snakes are ones that are raised in captivity. They're easier to handle because they don't know anything else. Those are the kinds you should keep as pets."

"And wild-captured?" Alice asked. "They were in the wild?"

"Yes, and then someone captured them. They're more dangerous to keep as pets."

"Were there any of those?" G-Mom asked.

"One," Ellis said, blowing gently on Juan's soft hair. "Big Monte."

CHAPTER 14

Alice walked her fingers slowly down Zebby's rib cage. She was afraid Ellis had been correct: Some of Zebby's ribs were broken. He still hadn't climbed to his feet, and he still seemed to have trouble breathing. The bite mark on his left shoulder was ugly and raw. The boa had gouged a dark red wound in his shoulder. She gently tickled his ear and whispered that she loved him.

It was noon and still raining. The apartment had become quiet. G-Mom dozed in the recliner. Carmen had been able to sit up enough to have the baby propped in her arms. Now they both slept, Carmen snoring lightly now and then, while the other three, Kuru, Ellis, and Day, stayed up on the roof, trying their best to get someone's attention.

Her job, at least as it was outlined in a brief meeting when Kuru and Day had returned with an armful of mismatched groceries, was to organize their supplies. She hadn't gotten very far. Or rather, there wasn't very far to get. They only had a day's, maybe two days,' supply. After that it was anyone's guess what they would eat. At least, she thought, they had plenty of water. They couldn't drink the floodwater – it was filled with gasoline and sewage – but the system they had organized for gathering rain worked effectively.

Shelter.

Check, she told herself.

Water, check. Food, check – for now.

She leaned over and kissed Zebby's bristly cheek. Zebby grunted softly.

After a while she stood and did the rounds. That's what they called snake patrol. Every twenty minutes or so someone was designated to go around the apartment and check to make sure no snake had wiggled its way inside. G-Mom had insisted on it. The door was shut. The windows, except the ones with a sheer drop-off on the side of the building, were also shut. Alice doubted a snake could get inside now, but it was worth checking anyway. She still could not believe the horror of seeing the snake wound around Zebby. The sheer smoothness of the attack, the efficiency, made her feel creepy inside her skin.

G-Mom came awake, looked right at her, then went back to sleep. Alice smiled. G-Mom was quite a character. Moving around the apartment, Alice checked on Carmen and the baby. Carmen opened her eyes.

"How are you feeling?" Alice asked.

"Better," Carmen said. "I'm actually hungry for the first time in a long while."

"I'll get you something. How's your neck?"

"Still hurts, but it's okay. How's Zebby?"

"I think some of his ribs are broken."

"Poor thing."

"I have half a doughnut here and some cheese and ham slices. Does any of that sound good?"

"A piece of doughnut is fine."

"It's probably stale," Alice said, carrying it over to Carmen. "But they still taste pretty good."

Carmen took the doughnut piece. Alice sat down at the far end of the couch.

"I'm Alice, by the way," she said. "We haven't really met officially."

"I'm Carmen."

"You fell and hurt your neck?"

Carmen nodded. She shot her hand to her neck as soon as she did that.

"It feels like it was wrenched, but it's getting better, I think. It just needed rest."

"Where's your mom?"

"She was working when the flood came on. And we haven't been able to make any contact."

"Everything is shut down," Alice agreed. "You'd think someone would come by."

"They will eventually, I guess. The water can't stay at this level forever."

"We should be okay. We have water. That's the main thing."

"We can always eat the snakes," Carmen said, smiling.

She looked down at baby Juan. He had started to wake. His hands moved in little orbits, but his eyes hadn't yet opened. She let him grab her index finger with his tiny hand. That seemed to quiet him.

"They should report back soon," Alice said, pointing her chin at the roof.

"It's going to be dark again before we know it. We don't have a flashlight? I can't believe we can't find one in this entire building."

"We have the flashlight, but not the batteries."

"That's really lame. You know what I keep thinking? I keep wondering if maybe this isn't the end of the world, you know? It could be. Maybe the whole world is ending and we don't know it."

"Don't go freaky on me," Alice said. "It's just a levee breaking."

"I know. But I've been thinking about it. How would you know if the world had ended? What if that's the reason we haven't seen any boats or helicopters?"

Alice looked at Carmen, trying to read her.

"I think the safer assumption to make is that we're just trapped here a little while."

"I know, I know," Carmen said. "My mother always

says I let my imagination run away with me. Don't think I'm nutty."

"I don't."

Carmen kissed the baby's head.

"I'm sorry about Zebby," she said.

"Me, too."

Then Alice heard the others coming down from the roof. They came quickly, but not in the panicked run she had heard before. They clomped down the stairs and then swung into the apartment, closing the door behind them. They carried another spaghetti pot full of water.

"We saw a helicopter," Kuru said. "It buzzed by, but it wasn't that close. It looked like a news copter."

"Where are the police?" Carmen asked. "It's weird we haven't seen the police at all."

"They may be around. We just haven't seen them," Day said. "I think we should try to get to the ground level to see if anything's moving down there."

"Go to the first floor?" Alice asked.

"Just to survey the surroundings," Day said. "Just to make sure things haven't changed and we don't know about it. There could be boats out on the street, and we wouldn't necessarily know it. The boats could stay right next to the buildings and maybe we couldn't see them from the roof."

"It's getting dark," Ellis said. "We should do it tomorrow morning if nothing has changed."

"Is it still raining?" Carmen asked.

"It's raining harder than ever," Kuru reported. "It's crazy."

"How's Zebby doing?" Ellis asked, kneeling next to the pig. "How you doing, boy?"

"Not great," Alice said. "He's not acting like himself."

"Poor little pork chop," Ellis said, petting him.

Then the building gave an enormous grinding sound. Alice held her breath. It was the loudest sound so far. The plate of remaining doughnuts slid slowly across the table. Something smashed in the kitchen. Zebby made an alarmed squeal, and G-Mom made a short, gargled sound and then sat forward.

No one moved. Alice looked around the small circle of people. The building was going over. Maybe not this minute, and maybe not in the next day or two, but the water had chopped away at the foundation and it was no longer solid. The building listed slightly to the left, its top leaning against the French Shoe Polish building. If you put a marble on the floor, she realized, it would have rolled at a good pace right across the apartment.

"We've got to get out of this building," Kuru said, her facial expression paused while she listened. "It's going to slide right down."

"In the morning we should go," Day said. "We should make a run for it."

"Run where?" Ellis asked. "Run how?"

No one answered. Alice stood and went to Zebby. She wasn't going to leave Zebby no matter what. No one could make her do that.

"Chess is the only game where there's no luck involved," Ellis said, his eyes fixed on the chessboard. "It's all skill. You can't blame anything if you lose. Win or lose, it's all on you."

"What about checkers?" Kuru asked.

"Checkers, too. Chinese or regular. All skill. Most games have luck. You introduce a ball, it's luck. You introduce teammates, passing, anything at all, and luck enters into it. Not chess, though. Chess is pure."

Day moved his bishop diagonally across the board. Ellis had seen it coming and countered it by sliding a pawn up to chase the bishop away. *Piece of cake*, he thought.

"What about boxing or something like that?" Alice asked.

She sat next to Kuru. They all sat at the table, the candlelight illuminating a tiny circle in the darkness. No one moved away casually. *Not with the snakes around*, Ellis thought. Not with Big Monte patrolling the hallways.

"Someone can trip," he said. "Someone can break a thumb on a perfectly solid punch, then they can no longer fight. All sorts of things can happen. It's random. I'm telling you, chess is the ultimate test of skills."

Day kept advancing his knight on the other side of the bishop. Day was too aggressive most of the time, Ellis knew. Day wanted a quick kill, which was not a good tactical approach in chess. Chess required patience. If you forced things, they usually failed to work out. If you waited, on the other hand, you could usually spot a deficiency in your opponent's game. That's how Ellis played. He was a counterpuncher.

"If we started early in the morning and waded..." Carmen said from the couch.

"We can't wade," Alice said. "Not with G-Mom and the baby."

"Maybe not all of us then," Carmen said. "Maybe we send out a rescue party."

Ellis thought that was a bad idea, but he didn't say anything. He castled to the right, moving his king two spaces and his rook to the other side. That was something Day hated to do. Day considered it a waste of a move, but Ellis knew better. You had to castle, the earlier the better. That was a cautious approach, but the smart one, too.

"I think they know where we are," Kuru said. "The authorities do, I mean. But maybe they can't get to us. Or maybe there are other people in worse shape."

"Maybe they've just forgotten us," Day said. "Maybe this part of town isn't a top priority."

"You mean they know we're here, but don't care?" Alice asked.

Day shrugged. He moved his bishop again. Ellis easily fended it off with a pawn. Day ignored the power of pawns. Pawns ruled, Ellis thought. They moved forward step by step, narrowing the noose with each push forward. People liked to concentrate on the big pieces, but the pawns won the day most times.

"If we walked away from the river, eventually we'd reach dry ground," Kuru said. "That just stands to reason, doesn't it?"

"But it's dangerous walking in the water," Alice said. "There could be all kinds of stuff in the water. I'm not talking about the snakes now, I'm talking about broken glass, or rusty metal. You don't know what you'd be getting into."

"We can't stay here," Kuru said. "The building is going to go over."

"Don't say that," G-Mom said, the baby on her lap. "Don't even give those words air."

"G-Mom, it's true," Kuru said. "I don't like it any more than you do, but it's true. The foundation is undermined."

"If we send out a party to look for help," Ellis said,

"that leaves us short-handed here. If anything happens with a snake, or anything else, then we're in trouble."

That was chess, Ellis realized. You made your moves, calculated your risks, then made cautious advances. People liked to overlook the obvious, pretend it didn't matter, but Ellis knew better. You had to proceed in an intelligent way. If you didn't, you were sure to lose.

"I say we make an assessment in the morning," Ellis said. "Maybe it will stop raining and maybe the water will start going down. We can't know what the conditions will be like twelve hours from now. The main thing is to get through the night safely."

"What about the building?" Kuru asked.

"We'll have to trust that it will hold up. We don't have anywhere to go. There's nothing else we can do right now."

No one said anything after that. Kuru took the baby from G-Mom and sat him on the edge of the table. He looked like a chubby little Buddha sitting there, Ellis thought. He reached over and ran his knuckle gently against the baby's cheek. He loved how soft a baby's skin could be. He loved that a lot.

SURVIVAL TIP #4

As a rule of thumb, be wary of changing location in a survival situation. Sometimes it may be the best course of action to seek new ground, but often it is recommended that the survivalist remain where she or he is until the authorities can locate her or him. During a crisis in an urban or semi-urban environment especially, the authorities are likely to be well aware of the stranded party's circumstances and will typically have plans in place to effect a rescue. By moving, the survivalist only makes the rescue effort more complicated. In most cases, in other words, stay with the capsized boat, the stalled vehicle, the remote cabin — unless it is absolutely necessary to move. Be patient and make yourself visible to potential search parties.

CHAPTER 15

Day stepped into the water and held his breath at the shock of cold. The water came up to his chest. It felt strange to be standing in the bakery with the water pressing against him. He looked at Kuru and Ellis. They still remained on the stairs looking down like kids on Christmas morning gazing at a Christmas tree. It might almost have been funny under different circumstances, he thought.

"How is it?" Kuru asked.

"Cold," Day said.

"Can you make it over to the door?" Ellis asked.

"Not sure yet. You can't see your feet, so it's hard to know where you're stepping," Day said, his hands held up near his chin like squirrel paws as he slowly slid his right foot forward. "You guys can hop in anytime you like."

"Let's see how you do making it to the door," Ellis said. "Then we'll see what's what."

"You two are a great help," Day said, still probing with his feet. "I think the water's moved things around."

"Probably did," Kuru agreed. "The door swings in, not out. You might get a rush of water when you open it, so be ready. And I put some flour bags against the door, so you might have to push them aside."

"It's still raining," Ellis said. "Hard to believe, but it is. Not as bad, though."

It had looked sunnier earlier when they had decided to test the waters, so to speak. That's what Day remembered. But sitting in an apartment on the second floor surrounded by a bunch of people was different from wading chest-deep across a flooded bakery. He didn't even want to think of Big Monte or the other snakes. Boas and pythons did just fine in water, he knew. They often hunted in water, so it did not make him happy to be wading through the jungle juice in the bakery. Besides, the water smelled funky and felt slimy. Nothing about the situation was particularly pleasant. He could only imagine what the street would be like.

"Wasn't there a boat over by the park?" Ellis asked. "Wasn't there one up on sawhorses?"

"It was a sailboat," Day said, still poking along. "It was pretty big."

"Wonder if we could get to that."

"It looked pretty beat up. It looked like one of those things people put in their backyards and then forget about."

"But at least it might float. It would be someplace to aim for," Kuru chimed in. "I know where you mean. It was painted a weird shade of blue, right?"

"Right," Ellis said. "Sky blue, kind of."

"This is so gross," Day said. "It stinks."

"You're almost there," Kuru said. "Keep going."

"Not sure what I'm supposed to see once I get on the street."

"We won't know until we know," Ellis said.

Day reached the bakery door. It was locked when he tried to pull it.

"Turn the thumb lock to the right," Kuru said. "It should work."

He turned it. He heard a solid click to indicate it had released. He reached down for the doorknob and turned it. Then he felt with his feet for the flour bags. He found them easily, but it took a long time to shove them aside. Finally, the door came back slowly, floating, it felt like, and he stepped back to give it room. The opening permitted more water to flow in, but it wasn't a tidal wave. It merely allowed a sigh of water to settle inside.

"Ta-da," he said.

"Now go out and look around," Ellis said. "Maybe you should make some noise to alert anyone who might be in the other buildings around here."

"What kind of noise?"

"Just anything, really. Just bang on stuff or yell."

"Let me look for a second to see what's going on."

Day stepped outside. *Waded* outside, he thought. Rain fell on his head and shoulders, but it nevertheless felt good to be out of the building. To be free of it. He took a few more steps out onto the sidewalk. It was easy to forget a world existed beyond the building, he reflected. He took a deep breath and slowly looked up and down the street. Everything was flooded, obviously, but it took a little while for him to absorb what that meant. Water covered the cars, for one thing, and their roofs lingered just at the surface of the water like seals or whales swimming by. The traffic light on Halston Street had toppled over and stared like a dead eye at him. Mrs. DuMont's flower boxes, her pride and joy, his mother always said, floated next to the next building's side. They had come loose and bobbled in the water like sugar cubes or playing dice.

"So?" Ellis called. "What's it like?"

"It's flooded."

"Duh," Ellis said. "How bad?"

"What do you mean, how bad? Real bad. Crazy bad," Day said, still looking around.

"Is it dangerous?" Kuru called. "Is the water running fast or anything like that?"

"Not too bad," Day answered, judging the water's force against his body. It did not really try to push him one way or the other.

"So should we come out and join you?" Ellis asked.

Day turned around and shrugged.

"You guys," he said, "it depends if we want to try to make it out. Or try to make it over to that boat near the park. Coming out here hasn't really changed anything. G-Mom and Carmen can't walk through this. Neither can Zebby. And we can't leave them alone, can we?"

"Probably not," Ellis said.

"Not with the snakes and everything," Kuru agreed. "Is there another building that might be better? Can you see anyplace that might give us better security?"

"Not really. I could probably make it over to the parking garage, but that would be cold at night and dark. It wouldn't be much of a camp."

"Could we make it to Jenson's Market?" Ellis asked, mentioning the corner store they used. That had been part of the reason for coming out in the first place and they had all but forgotten it. "For batteries or something?"

"I can't tell for sure. We could make a try."

"Old Man Jenson won't be happy if people go into his store," Kuru said.

"Maybe he's not around," Day said. "Hold on. I'm wading back to you."

He passed through the bakery faster going back. When he climbed onto the stairs, Ellis stepped away.

"You reek!" Ellis said.

"Sorry," Day said. "That water's not exactly French perfume, you know."

"It's ripe," Kuru agreed.

"So what do we want to do?" Day asked, conscious of his smell and the water oozing off his body. "We could probably make it down to Jenson's Market. That's on the corner, so once we reached it we could look down a cross street. Or we could try to make it to that boat near the park, or we could just stay where we are."

"I think we should try for the market. One way or the other, that will help us figure out what's what," Ellis said.

"The boat doesn't make any sense, because we don't even know if it's still there," Kuru said, her hand to her face, Day understood, to block his odor. "It might have floated away, if it floated. And like you said, or someone said, G-Mom isn't going anywhere."

"But if the building keeps sliding down," Ellis said, "we're done for."

"Let's go down to the store," Day said. "If we do it fast, we can be down and back before anyone needs us. It shouldn't take long."

"I don't want to run into Mr. Jenson," Kuru said. "He's not in a good mood on a regular day. This flooding won't have helped."

"Well, whatever," Ellis said. "He may have some stuff we need. He may not even be around. We can try it and turn back."

Day nodded and stepped back into the water.

"Come on," he said over his shoulder.

"I can't believe I'm going in that water," Kuru said. "And no showers afterward. Nothing."

"It won't be so bad," Ellis said, stepping in with Day. "You can stay if you want and we'll go."

"I'm coming," Kuru said, and splashed as she stepped into the water.

Day waded toward the road just as he had done a few minutes before. The other two followed.

Alice heard something in the storage room. She wasn't one hundred percent positive it was *the* storage room, the place where they had put the snake that had hurt Zebby, but it seemed to be the likeliest place. She stood for a long time looking at the door to the closet.

She wasn't supposed to be alone. That was policy; they had all agreed on it. But she had ducked out of the apartment to check on the scouting party, curious where they had gone, if they had come back, and so forth, and she had found herself standing at the top of the stairs, the storage closet immediately to her left. The ridiculous door even said STORAGE, although the writing had long since lost its hold on the door and she had to read the empty places where the letters used to be.

It read: TO AG. The *S* and *R* and *E* had faded away.

It was afternoon. Early afternoon. She didn't like how long Kuru and Day and Ellis had been away. They had all agreed that they wouldn't take off on any long-term mission unless they informed the apartment people of their intentions, but maybe they had gotten caught in something. Alice didn't know and neither did G-Mom or Carmen, so they had all become increasingly worried until Alice consented to go out and look.

Just to the top of the landing, you hear me? G-Mom had said emphatically. *No farther. You come right back here.*

That's exactly what she intended to do, so that when she reached the top of the landing and stared down the damp staircase at the flooded first floor below, she had every intention of hustling back to the apartment to report her findings.

No sign of them, she imagined herself saying. *Weird, huh?*

That's when something went *bump* in the storage closet.

It was a good, solid sound. It wasn't anything she could mistake. It didn't come from the building shifting, or from the mops and brooms inside suddenly deciding to slide sideways. No, this was an *animate* sound. Animate was a good vocab word, one that meant *verb: to bring to life*, or *adjective: alive or having life*, and the word certainly fit the noise behind the door.

Something was moving around in there. And she was fascinated.

Not that she was going to open the door. Never that. But the thought of the snake looped over the shelves inside, waiting, its backward-pointing teeth glinting, made her surprisingly . . .

Intrigued. It was a little like a nightmare you have as you're waking on a soft summer morning, and you think of the horrid elements of the dream contrasted to the gentleness of the waking, and you are the tiniest bit *intrigued*. You allow yourself to stay asleep, even when you know you could wake up and be done with it, because something about the nightmare is, well, intriguing. It just is. And if you're lucky, she thought, you hang on the edge of dream and waking, indulging in the frightening images, exploring while simultaneously appalled by what you might see.

That's what the snake in the storage room meant to her. Just that.

She put her ear to the door. She heard something slow and stealthy moving behind the wooden barrier.

"I hear you," she whispered to it. "You can't fool me."

She put her hand on the doorknob.

"Want me to let you out?" she whispered. "Want to come out and play?"

And that was nuts, she knew. She shuddered at the thought of the snake slipping out of the closet, its wedge-shaped head leading the pile of spine. She wiggled the doorknob, just to have sound, and then put her ear to the door again to see if the snake reacted. No noise came from inside.

Clever, she thought. *It's very clever.*

She let the doorknob rest and turned away from the door. She must be crazy, she told herself. She flexed her knees and looked once more down the stairway to the first floor. Water caught the dull sunshine and turned the reflection milky. *No sign of them. Nothing to report.*

"What did you see?" G-Mom asked when she came back into the apartment.

"No sign of them," Alice said, moving over to pet Zebby.

"You were gone a long time," Carmen said. "What were you doing out there?"

"Nothing. Just listening to see if I could hear anything."

"And did you?" Carmen asked.

Alice shook her head. The baby started crying then. Alice felt glad to have the noise. She didn't like thinking about her hand on the doorknob of the storage closet, or of the sound of the snake moving behind the door. It sounded like a mop head splashing quietly on the floor, like water releasing and being drawn back to its source.

CHAPTER 16

Kuru followed through the water, staying directly in line with the two boys. She hated wading through water, hated not being able to see her feet, hated not being sure what she stepped on at any given moment. The street outside the bakery looked otherworldly. Rain kept falling and everything in the world had shifted or moved, it seemed, and you could not depend on anything being where you expected it to be.

Day led. Ellis took the middle and she brought up the rear. On a normal day, under normal circumstances, it would have taken less than a minute or two to walk to Jenson's Market. But not today. Not anytime in the near future, she imagined.

"Do you shop at Jenson's Market?" Ellis asked.

"Prices are too high," she said, still wading. "And Old Man Jenson is a nasty thing. He was mean to G-Mom once."

"He's pretty gross," Day agreed. "But it's convenient."

"We do our shopping at the BJ's. We buy in bulk."

"Old Man Jenson performed a citizen's arrest on Kyle Ellison," Day said. "He has a samurai sword he keeps on hooks by the register and he held it right to Kyle's neck. He said Kyle had shoplifted something, but Kyle swears he didn't."

"I've never seen the sword," Ellis said.

"Well, he has one," Day assured him. "It was his dad's from World War Two. His dad got it off a dead Japanese soldier."

"A samurai sword? He's too fat to use a samurai sword," Kuru said.

"That guy eats," Day said. "I mean, he packs it down. He always has a bag of something open and his fingers are always oily."

"Some samurai," Kuru said.

"No one said he *was* a samurai," Ellis said. "We said he has a samurai sword, that's all."

Kuru watched the boys step up on something, then lower back into the water. At least the water didn't deepen. It stayed at chest level, grosser than gross, but it was manageable. Of course, it also depended on whether you stepped into a hole, or into anything deeper. Then you would have trouble. Plus, the water was cold, bone cold, and she didn't think you could wade in it for long. Pretty soon it would leach the warmth right out of your body. The whole thing was a mess.

"Here we go," Day said, finally arriving at Jenson's Market. "The security gate is down. There's no one there."

"Knock and see," Ellis said.

Day knocked. He yelled, "Helllloooooo?" too, but no one answered. Kuru watched him turn away and shrug. At the same time Old Man Jenson opened the door to the store. He wore a pair of fishing waders and carried the samurai sword in his hand. The samurai sword had a braided tassel dangling from the handgrip. It looked sharp and deadly.

"What do you want?" he asked.

For the first time Kuru realized Old Man Jenson was not that old. He merely looked old. His hair was thin on top, and grayish red, but his fat face was younger than she recollected. He had a huge discoloration on the back of his right hand. Maybe it was a rash, or maybe it was a birthmark, but it drew her eye. He acted old, though, grumpy and out of sorts. Funny how people got their nicknames.

"We wanted to get some batteries for a flashlight," Day said.

"A hundred bucks," Old Man Jenson said, his voice flat and breathy.

"What?" Ellis asked.

"I said a hundred bucks."

"Are you crazy?" Day said.

"You don't want them, it's okay with me. We're in flood conditions, in case you didn't notice."

"You want a hundred bucks for a couple batteries?" Ellis asked. "You must be crazy."

"You see anybody else selling batteries around here? It's what's called a seller's market. Batteries are rare right now. You're welcome to go to another store."

"You know we can't do that," Kuru said. "Why do you want to be like that?"

Old Man Jenson didn't say anything. He simply regarded them through the crosshatch of the security gate.

"Are you hearing any reports?" Ellis asked. "About when someone's going to get in here? Or when the water is going down?"

"Nope. No reports."

"You haven't heard them, or you won't tell us?" Day asked.

"You want the batteries or not?" Jenson asked.

"Wow, you are one greedy man," Kuru said. "Won't even help out neighbors."

"You're not my neighbors. You're just flies landing on a cube of sugar."

"Let's get out of here," Kuru said.

"Fifty dollars," Jenson said. "Take it or leave it."

"We'll leave it," Ellis said. "Have a nice day, Jenson."

Jenson shrugged and shut the door. Kuru looked at the other two.

"I cannot believe what just happened," she said.

"So much for neighbor helping neighbor," Day said. "That guy is warped."

"He had the samurai sword," Ellis said. "That thing looked pretty cool."

"Lethal," Kuru agreed. "Now what?"

"Let's just look down the cross street and see what we can see. Is there any other store nearby?" Day asked.

"No, I don't think so," Ellis said. "We can visit the boat if that still makes sense."

"The boat's too far," Kuru said. "We should head back after we check the cross street."

"She's right," Day said. "We're just going to have to wait it out."

"With Big Monte," Ellis said.

"Yes, with Big Monte," Day said.

Kuru took the lead and circled the opening of Jenson's Market so she could look down the cross street. There wasn't much to see. Water spread everywhere, all the way down to the river, from what she could tell. She spotted a few distinguishing landmarks – a sizeable oak tree she liked, a swing set behind a crumbled old house, an oil tank on metal legs – but otherwise things were submerged. Nothing really had changed, yet everything had changed. It was peculiar.

The rain refused to let up as they turned around for the apartment house. It made a gentle patter on the surface of the floodwater. Suddenly, Kuru heard a beating sound. It came fast, gaining in volume, and it took her a moment to realize it was a helicopter. It came quickly and passed almost directly over them. Kuru saw a soldier sitting in the doorway. He waved. Or maybe it was a woman, she couldn't tell, because whoever it was wore a uniform.

"They know we're here," Ellis said. "At least we know that now."

"How do we know that?" Day asked.

"Because they didn't stop. If we had been a big surprise to them, they would have circled around and come back to tell us something. But they know we're here. I guarantee it."

"Glad you can guarantee it," Kuru said. "I'm not so sure."

"They probably had to get people in more critical conditions. They'll get us tomorrow. We just have to make it through one more night."

Kuru regarded Ellis. The kid was pretty shrewd. The

whole chess-playing thing worked for him. It seemed to influence every part of his life.

"He's probably right," Day said. "He usually is about stuff like this."

"Take it to the bank," Ellis said, trying to sound like a rapper. He only managed to sound ridiculous. Still, Kuru laughed. It had been a while since she had last laughed. "To the bank," Ellis said again, but this time it wasn't funny. It was just stupid, but she didn't mind. She kept laughing anyway.

Carmen heard the helicopter and looked out the window. She couldn't see it. But Alice hopped to the kitchen window and caught a glimpse of it as it continued over the city. Alice hooted a little with her face still pointing toward the window. The hoot woke G-Mom, who simply turned to get more comfortable in the recliner. Carmen kept the baby in her arms.

"They saw us," Alice said. "I'm positive."

"How could you tell?"

"I saw one of the soldiers in the doorway or hatch or

whatever you call it. He made an okay sign with his index finger and thumb. You know."

Carmen watched Alice make the okay sign. She couldn't help but make it back.

"It's about time someone came looking for us," Carmen said. "Not to sound too annoying about it, but come on. We've been here a couple days already."

"I think it's big," Alice said, "bigger than we might know. I bet they've been crazy busy rescuing people."

"You're probably right," Carmen said. "I suppose I sound ungrateful. I didn't mean to be."

"No, I get what you're saying. It's all pretty weird."

Carmen tucked the baby closer. Her neck felt better. She liked Alice. Alice was friendly and helpful. She checked the apartment against snakes on a regular schedule and she brought food to the baby whenever she was asked. Nevertheless, Carmen didn't know what it was, but she couldn't quite get a lock on Alice's background. Every time she asked a direct question of Alice, Alice managed to avoid answering it. When she asked about the band, or about school, Alice's answers didn't stack up. Carmen had started to think that Alice didn't have an address, or a place to call home. Maybe she lived out of her car, or maybe she lived somewhere in the abandoned building next door, but whatever it was seemed to embarrass Alice. Alice didn't volunteer anything, that was for sure, but she asked plenty of questions about Carmen and her life. It was strange.

But one thing was sure: She loved Zebby. She spent a lot of time on her knees next to the pig, giving him bites of food whenever he would accept them. Having a pig didn't exactly fit the profile of a homeless person, but then again, it didn't fit the profile of a rocker either. Alice's situation felt muddy to Carmen.

"How's Zebby doing?" Carmen asked, mostly to make conversation.

"He'll be okay, I think. He's still in shock a little."

"I guess we all are. So what will you do about your car? When the flood's over, I mean."

Alice didn't look at her, Carmen noted. She kept her eyes down on Zebby.

"I guess get it towed or something. Maybe the town will just take it. If I can take the tags off it, maybe

I'll just abandon it. I doubt it will start after all that water."

"What kind was it again?" Carmen asked.

"A Subaru Impreza."

"Good car?" Carmen asked, registering that Alice had said a Volkswagen before. A Jetta.

"Pretty good. I guess not good enough."

Carmen waited a moment before she asked the next question.

"Are you homeless, Alice?" she asked, deliberately softening her voice.

Carmen couldn't tell if she had overstepped or not. Part of her wanted to suck the question back in because it was none of her business, but another part, a deeper part, didn't like thinking of Alice being all alone. She watched Alice closely. Alice didn't take her eyes of Zebby. At the same time, Carmen realized her own fear of the shower curtain counted for nothing compared to Alice's situation.

"Not really," she answered finally. "Kind of between homes."

"Were you living in your car or something?"

Alice didn't answer. She shrugged and kept petting Zebby.

"I'm sorry if I am too nosy," Carmen said. "I know I can be at times, but I didn't mean to be in this case. Honest. I just like you and I was worried about you."

"I'm okay," Alice said. "But thanks."

"So were you going someplace when your car got trapped?"

"To my brother's," Alice said. "In Iowa."

"You don't live with your parents?"

"Not anymore."

"Okay," Carmen said. "Sorry. I didn't mean to pry."

"It's all right. My brother is in the service. The army. He has room for me."

"Good. I'm glad to hear that."

"They didn't want me living there anymore," Alice said. "It's a long, dismal story."

"That's your business. Sorry."

Alice didn't say anything. She pet Zebby slowly and carefully, as if getting his hair properly combed was the most important thing she had ever undertaken. It reminded Carmen of a little kid playing with sand on a beach.

"They don't like Zebby, either," Alice said. "They wanted to give him away."

"To the humane society?"

"To a dog food company," Alice said, and it took Carmen a second to realize it was a joke. "No, they knew a guy who had a farm. A friend of my dad's. They wanted to put him out to pasture with the guy. I told them to forget it. Zebby is my friend. Turns out he would have been saved a lot of trouble if he had just gone out on the farm. He would have avoided a snake bite and some cracked ribs."

"Will your brother let him live with you?"

She shrugged. "I guess we'll find out, won't we, Zebby?" she asked her pet.

"I don't know if we're going to be much better off than your situation," Carmen said. "I think this apartment building will be condemned."

"I hope for your sake it's not."

Carmen didn't know what she felt. Everything seemed jumbled up, but at the same time she didn't think a new start would be a bad idea. At least their apartment wasn't flooded the way Kuru and G-Mom's was flooded. At least she and her mom and Juan had that much going for them.

"How did you know I was between places to live?" Alice asked. "I thought I did a pretty good job of covering myself."

"Just a vibe. And you changed the make of your car when you mentioned it this last time."

"I'm hitchhiking, actually," Alice said. "That's why."

"With a pig?"

Alice shrugged again.

"I didn't say it was easy," she said.

CHAPTER 17

Ellis saw Big Monte as soon as they stepped through the doorway of the apartment building. Big Monte was unmistakable. He was huge, for one thing, and more alert than any of the other snakes. At least that's the impression he gave. He was a mottled green-and-black color and thick – thick as a leg, thick as a pot roast. Big Monte's head appeared long and smooth, a bicycle seat, and his eyes, unblinking, flickered with cunning. Big Monte understood a few things. That was clear with just a glance.

He lay on the staircase in between the safety of the apartment and the sodden ugliness of the bakery level. To get to dryness, to get back to the second floor, they had to get past Big Monte.

"That's him, isn't it?" Kuru asked.

Her voice sounded shaky. Day nodded. Ellis nodded, too. Ellis couldn't say if Kuru's shaky voice came from fear or from being frozen. It was horribly cold in the water and each one of them had taken on a constant tremble. They had no choice. That had to get out or freeze.

"That's him," Ellis said. "Big Monte."

"He's horrid," Kuru said, her voice chattering.

"He's pretty magnificent, really," Ellis said. "He's a killing machine."

"Is he going to come into the water after us?" she asked.

"Probably not," Day said. "He'll probably just stand his ground on the stairs."

"And if we go near him . . . ?" Kuru asked.

"It's not a good idea to go near him," Ellis said. "He'll be territorial. And he's probably a little panicked with all this cold water. Or maybe not. He was caught down in the Everglades."

"He lived wild," Day said. "Probably about ten years. Then he's been in captivity for about five more years. Maybe longer. You don't want to mess with him."

"What do we do now then?" Kuru asked. "We have to get past him."

"We should wait until he leaves," Ellis said. "Just wait and see what happens."

"It's too cold in the water," Day said. "We can't wait that long."

"We can throw some things at him and see if he'll move away."

"Why not try to kill him?" Kuru asked. "I mean, can't we do something like that?"

"With the ax we could, maybe. But if you missed and just wounded him, you'd be in a world of trouble."

Ellis studied the snake. If the snake wanted to, he could enter the water and disappear. He could go through the water faster than they could track him. Plus, he could hold his breath for a long time. Advantage, Big Monte. Once he was in the water, anything could happen, although Ellis still doubted Big Monte would have any interest in them. They were too big and too many. But if they backed him into a corner, or made him feel threatened, the result wouldn't be good. Not good at all.

"It's like a dragon tale out of a book," Kuru said. "He's a dragon guarding his hoard and we're the travelers trying to get past."

"We could throw some things at him and see how he reacts," Ellis said. "Just small things to get him thinking. We don't want to go to war with him."

"If he comes in the water . . ." Kuru started, but didn't finish.

"I'll grab some plates and things," Day said. "Grab things that are heavy enough to send out vibrations when they land. Snakes live with vibrations. Their hearing isn't much."

"They're deaf, pretty much," Ellis said. "Grab some pots, too."

"If he goes after one of us, will we be able to pull him off?" Kuru asked.

"Maybe, maybe not," Ellis said. "He's unbelievably strong. We had to handle him one time to put him in a larger cage. Teddy helped and we got tossed around until his brother showed up. If his brother hadn't come along, it wasn't going to be good."

"So maybe we should just leave him alone," Kuru said, clearly uncomfortable. "Maybe we should find somewhere else to be."

"Where?" Day asked. "We don't have anyplace to go. They're expecting us back."

Day sloshed into the bakery. Ellis stayed to keep an eye on Big Monte. Kuru didn't move one way or the other. Big Monte was Teddy's favorite, Ellis knew. After the tough guy who had bought him brought him back, Teddy had contacted a local zoo about Big Monte, but the zookeepers had not been too excited about the prospect of a large, wild-captured python. *Too unpredictable* is how they phrased it to Teddy. Ellis knew Teddy took the zoo's reluctance as a compliment. Big Monte was too crazy wild for a zoo, but he, Teddy, could handle him. That stoked Teddy whenever he mentioned it.

Day came back with an armful of glasses and small saucepans. He handed them out. It was easy enough to target around the snake, Ellis knew. But how the snake reacted was going to be anyone's guess. They wanted to discourage the snake without challenging him.

"Let's stand together so we look even bigger," Ellis said. "If he goes after any of us, then he has to coil around us all. We'll stand a better chance that way."

"He's tracking us," Kuru said. "His eyes follow us. He knows just what we're doing."

"Of course he is tracking us," Ellis agreed. "Wouldn't you if you were in his place? It's three against one. In the wild, he probably would have already taken off by now. Just disappeared in the underbrush."

"He's so big," Kuru said. "It's sick how big he is."

"He's double the size of the one we took off Zebby," Day said. "At least double."

"Big Monte is king of the jungle," Ellis said. "He's the beast."

Then he lobbed a pan near the giant snake. The pan made a loud noise when it landed, but the snake didn't move in the least. Day threw a glass that shattered in a thousand pieces. Kuru threw another pan and this one hit the snake at the midpoint of his body. Big Monte moved a little at that. He flickered to life and coiled slightly.

"He's coming to," Day said. "He's probably cold and a little sluggish. Hate to wake him."

"Should we hit him, or just land things close?" Kuru asked.

"You can hit him. Just don't chuck it at him hard. Easy does it," Day said.

Ellis couldn't read the snake. Most snakes, he figured, would have already been in retreat. But not Big Monte. Big Monte stayed on the staircase with his body rolled together like a fist. Ellis had read a lot about snakes, but you could never know everything. Besides, snakes had personalities. Some proved to be docile and nearly stupefied, while others, like Big Monte, had a chip on their shoulders. Big Monte didn't take anything from anyone.

"Oh, I can't stand it when they move," Kuru said, her eyes fixed on Big Monte. "Creeps me right out."

"It's kind of beautiful, really," Ellis said, tossing a plate near the tail of the snake. "I think it is, anyway."

"Powerful," Day said, his voice clipped a little as he threw a pan toward the snake's head. "All muscle. That's how they look to me."

Kuru's voice suddenly went up an octave.

"Is he coming into the water?" she asked. "He's coming into the water, isn't he?"

"Don't panic," Day said. "It's okay. He's got to come into the water to pass us."

"Let's just back off," Kuru said. "This is crazy."

Ellis watched carefully, trying to read the snake's attitude. *What an amazing creature*, he thought. Big Monte was powerful and precise in everything he did. He uncurled slowly, but really, when you analyzed it, he simply let his head fall with gravity toward the water. He became limp and rigid at the same time, if that were possible, like a hand lowering to come back up in a punch. His middle coils simply floated down off the riser, and his tail trembled a bit as it went free from the balusters. You could be mesmerized by a snake, Ellis saw, by the fluidity of the movement. You watched the center of the snake, marveling at its solidity, and in the process you lost track of the head. Then the head came toward you, jaws wide, gums and mouth roof white with a black line across the lips, and the snake hit with such violence that it could puncture a hole through the fender of a car. Sometimes, Ellis knew, the force of the bite alone stopped the heart of a rabbit or small mammal, exploded the vessels and eyeballs of its victims into a balloon-like pop even before the snake coiled over it and crushed it.

All of that passed through his mind in an instant.

And then the snake put its head in the water and started moving rapidly at them.

Carmen heard the scream through the building, through the rugs and wooden floor, through the water that drenched everything, through the couch and the soft body of the baby, Juan. The scream went up and up and up, and she saw the tone register in G-Mom's expression. No one said anything. But Alice jumped to her feet, her movement so sudden it made Zebby grunt and try to get to his. He stumbled a little and then found his equilibrium, and that would have been a triumphant moment in any other situation, but not now. Now he looked like he wanted to run, and Carmen didn't blame him.

"That's Kuru!" G-Mom said, her voice betraying more alarm as she deciphered her granddaughter's voice. "She's downstairs."

"I'm going to check on her," Alice said. "Watch Zebby, please."

"Hurry," G-Mom said.

"I'll go, too," Carmen said. "You have the baby, G-Mom."

The sound of Kuru's voice made it impossible to stay in the apartment. Carmen had to help. That was all there was to it. The soreness in her neck no longer mattered. It had all come down to this, she knew.

Alice tore open the door and clumped down the hallway, her big boots impossibly solid. Carmen did her best to follow.

The scream came again. It came over and over. Something horrible had happened to Kuru, Carmen understood. She had never heard anyone scream at that level before. There was no mistaking it for anything but life and death in the balance.

"What is it?" Alice yelled.

Then apparently she saw.

"Oh, geez!" she said, and she rushed down the stairs.

When Carmen made it to the top of the stairs, she looked down and couldn't at first make out what she saw. Bodies, certainly. And water thrashing around. The afternoon had grown tired and the sun that came in weakly illuminated the scene. She stood for a long ten-count before she saw the snake twined around Kuru's body. Before she saw Ellis and Day pulling at the snake.

Then she met Kuru's eyes with hers. It happened only for an instant and she could not say with absolute certainty that it happened at all. But it felt like it did. She saw Kuru come up for air and she saw Kuru's eyes go soft, not wide and alarmed as Carmen would have expected. No, Kuru had given up, had acknowledged the superior strength of the snake, and she appeared almost calm in her surrender. Kuru was done. She was *done*.

Carmen went down the stairs as fast as she could. Her neck hurt and her body felt unused to movement, but she had to help. She had to do what she could. The snake looked endless in its coils. It looked heavy and dense and it reminded her, for a flash, of a long, knitted scarf on a cold day. It wrapped around Kuru's throat and shoulders, around her waist and arms, and she watched as Ellis pulled at the snake's tail, trying to free Kuru, but the snake simply jerked and writhed and yanked Ellis back and forth. Day had his hand on the snake's head, right behind the skull, but he couldn't seem to pry the teeth off Kuru's thigh. He kept shouting to *lengthen the snake, lengthen it,* but no one seemed to know what that meant.

Carmen stepped into the water and put her hands on the serpent. Alice already had her arms around the snake and her cheek down against it, trying for leverage.

"Where do you want me?" Carmen asked, but no one answered.

She went next to Ellis and tried to help him pull the tail in the reverse direction the coils had taken around Kuru.

"Hurry," Ellis said.

Carmen pulled until her neck hurt. She pulled after that, too, but she could not get the image of Kuru's expression out of her mind. Done. Kuru was done.

CHAPTER 18

Moments before, Kuru watched the snake dip into the water. He looked, she thought, almost as if he wanted a drink. But then the rest of the body followed the head into the surface film, and instead of going under, accepting the liquidity of water, the snake simply stretched out. His body undulated and the last of his huge coils came off the stairs. Then she had concentrated on the wake. Yes, the snake caused a wake when he passed through the water, a triangle of motion breaking away from the head.

She backed away. She looked around furiously for something with which to fend the snake away. They had promised her that the snake had no interest in them. They were too big, too many, and the snake could not eat them anyway. What would he gain by attacking? That was her thought. Even as the snake shivered closer she wondered what he was doing.

"Look out!" Day yelled.

"Stay together," Ellis said.

As if that were a magical incantation, Kuru thought. As if that made any difference to the snake. If they just stayed together, he seemed to think, the snake would go on his way.

"He's coming this way!" Kuru yelled.

The next thing that happened seemed inevitable. It seemed as though she had been waiting for it to happen her entire life. The snake did not turn right or left, did not even hesitate. He swam directly at her and then submerged. A peculiar silence entered the room, an instantaneous waiting, and then the snake hit her.

It nearly knocked her down. He bit into the meaty part of her thigh, jammed into it, and forced her to take a step backward. She screamed. It was no big scream, because although it hurt to be bitten, it was not unendurable. She felt the snake's mouth on her leg, but that didn't mean it was the end of the world. She had suffered injuries in sports, had the usual assortment of breaks and sprains, so she was not a sissy when it came to physical pain.

But then the snake began to froth.

That was the right word for it: *frothing*. The snake began to pull itself forward from his purchase on her leg. His body curled and tossed, seeking a hold, and at last he looped up and grabbed around her waist. Even that, *even that*, did not seem horrible. She still had a sense that they could pull Big Monte off her, unwind him as they had unwound the snake that had bitten Zebby. Yes, the snake was enormous. She felt his weight being slowly transferred from the water onto her body, but it felt, at least in those first moments, as if she had been given something terribly heavy to carry. The weight was not in her arms, or supported by her hands, but clung to her entire body. The snake felt like the world's heaviest backpack. She staggered a little as he conquered more of her body.

And that's when it became terrifying.

What had started as a dreadfully fascinating encounter suddenly became genuinely perilous. The snake curled and rolled and without really understanding how he had performed his lock so easily, suddenly she knew she was trapped. The snake had his long body around her, strand by strand, and she felt his presence. Felt his attachment to her. A constrictor, she knew, did not simply begin squeezing. When its victim exhaled, the snake simply tightened, making each breath shorter, shallower, less and less satisfactory. Eventually, the prey could no longer expand its lungs to take in oxygen. Kuru understood that intellectually, but her body resisted by pumping more blood and demanding greater gulps of air.

She slipped and fell. She went under the water and that would have finished her, she knew, but Alice suddenly helped her to her feet. That made three people to pull the snake off her. What had Ellis said? How many people per how many feet of snake? She couldn't remember. But they were full-grown adults, probably, not young kids. The equation had too many variables.

Kuru wondered if she was about to die.

She tried to resist such a morbid thought, but it tightened on her just as the snake's coils constricted on her. *This is how I end,* she thought. For a moment she spotted

Carmen standing on the steps, slowly descending to help, and she wondered if Carmen could pull hard enough, if her neck would allow her to do so. That was a funny notion to have, she knew. With a snake squeezing her slowly, her mind went to Carmen's neck condition. Funny. The entire world was funny, when you thought about it, and she decided she did not hate the snake. Did not hate Big Monte. He was only trying to survive, just as they had, just as they had scurried up to the second-floor apartment, so why shouldn't the snake do his best to keep on living? It was only fair.

She fell again. And when she rose once more she felt the arms of a man around her.

Several men, actually. The men wore uniforms and they spoke rapidly, but not in panic, and a moment later the snake began to unwind. She heard a radio squawk and she heard someone say, a man's voice, that they should get the head free. Then she heard Ellis saying, *Big Monte, his name is Big Monte*, and that probably made no sense to anyone. A team, she realized. A team of rescuers had found them at last, and she couldn't say where they had come from, or how they knew what to do with the snake, but her breath started to pass more freely to her lungs. The snake stopped frothing and became a ribbon of muscle, a mottled length of heavy cordage. She fell when the snake's weight finally left her. Someone lifted her quickly and put her back on her feet.

"You okay?" a man in a uniform asked. "You all right?"

She nodded. She was. She was okay.

Ellis sat in the boat and listened to the radios buzz back and forth. That was the sound that filled every corner for a while. Radios clicking on and off, static, the burr of an electric connection just before voices came through. People talked quickly into the radios at their shoulders. They asked a lot of questions about the snakes. Clearly, they didn't like the idea of snakes roaming around. At the same time, Ellis knew they found the situation kind of interesting. It wasn't every day you ran into pythons or boas set loose in a flood. It was one thing to get people out of buildings, but quite another to release someone from a constrictor. Ellis saw it pumped up the rescue folks. It was a touch of drama.

"They were down in the basement," Ellis said to the man who piloted the boat. He had asked where they had been housed. The man relayed the information to someone somewhere else. Ellis wondered if Teddy eventually would get into trouble. He might. It was probably against the law to run a snake breeding business in the basement of an apartment building.

"Your parents have been crazy with worry," the man said. "We had to prevent them from trying to wade in here to rescue you. If they had known about the snakes, there's no way we could have stopped them."

The boat Ellis sat in was not large. It was an aluminum skiff, maybe fourteen feet long. The man who asked the questions had his body half turned around to manage the engine throttle. His name was Dave. His partner, at the bow, was named Lucille. They were National Guard members. They were going around evacuating people.

"How many snakes?" Dave asked.

"Around a dozen," Ellis said. "I think a dozen."

"A dozen," Dave said into the radio at his shoulder. Ellis heard someone reply, but he couldn't make out the words. He wondered what they would do about the snakes. Hunt them, he imagined. They had also said the buildings along his street were undermined. One had already collapsed about a quarter of a mile away. That was a danger in floods, Dave said, buildings going down. He said Jenson's Market would likely collapse, although the owner, Mr. Jenson, refused any offer of rescue. Eventually, they would have to condemn some of the buildings. That was for later, Dave said, once the water had withdrawn.

The boat eased slowly through the flood. They could not use the engine freely, Dave had already explained. Too many objects in the water, too much debris. They didn't want to bust off the propeller. They headed south, directly away from the Illinois River. Dave had told them all a rescue center had been set up in a high school gym. Ellis didn't recall the name of the high school, but he didn't really care. He was hungry and tired and cold.

"How much does a snake sell for, anyway?" Dave asked.

"Depends, I guess. A couple hundred. Sometimes a thousand if it's a really good specimen."

"Who knew?" Dave said, obviously surprised.

"They're good pets most of the time," Ellis said, feeling the need to defend them. "This was just a strange situation."

"Someone once told me they put a fetal monitor on a pregnant python's belly and the babies' hearts made a whirring sound. Not a beat, like a mammal's, but a whirring sound, like an engine revving up. Or like wind."

"I don't know about that," Ellis said. "It could be."

"Well, that's what I heard. Makes you wonder, doesn't it?"

"I guess."

"Not far now," Dave said, aiming the boat between two car roofs.

It was strange to float down roads and past buildings. But as they went, Ellis could tell the water became shallower. The water would draw back to the river, finally, and that water would go to the Mississippi River. The Mississippi would empty into the ocean somewhere in Louisiana, and Ellis wondered if a snake could travel that entire distance, eating along the way, picking off pets and rats and squirrels and traveling at night. Big

Monte, he thought, could make it. He had once read about a bull shark that had traveled up the Mississippi to the Ohio River all the way to Cincinnati. It had raided a fishing weir, and when they had finally caught it, they couldn't believe a shark had traveled through freshwater for hundreds of miles. If a shark could come up the river, he reflected, a python could probably go down the same watercourse.

For a while he dozed. He felt tremendously sleepy now. The boat rocked him and he held a green army blanket around him. When he woke now and then, coming up out of dreams to rejoin the world, he saw G-Mom and Kuru in a second boat. Carmen and the baby, too. He was in the boat with his brother, Day, and with Alice and Zebby. They puttered along, the water no longer a real obstacle. Rain still fell. Lucille said it was supposed to stop by the end of the day. Good weather, she said, was on its way.

Crash. Stranded. Stay Alive.

STAY ALIVE

CRASH

JOSEPH MONNINGER

STAY ALIVE

CRASH

SCHOLASTIC

Who will survive?

Before the plane crashed, before it became more than the sound of a mosquito up in the sky, a moose, a great northern Alaskan moose, stepped into the bright body of water called Long Lake. The moose appeared coated in copper; he had been rolling in dirt and mud to rid his ears and body of the mosquitoes that peppered him all day. He weighed thirteen hundred pounds and stood over seven feet high at the shoulder. He possessed a forty-inch-long leg and measured ten feet from tail to nose. As distant relatives, he counted the wapiti or North American elk, the caribou, the mule deer, and the whitetail in his family. He was a deer, the largest in the world, and on this summer evening, his pedicels – two small knots of soft tissue just forward of the ears – had pushed out into what became, over the long summer season, the trademark symbol of moose: palmate antlers.

He was the first animal to notice the plane.